Praise for
Carlton Mellick III

"Easily the craziest, wei[rd]... [obsc]ene writer in America."
—*GOTHIC MAGAZINE*

"Carlton Mellick III has the c[oolest ... and] the kinkiest fans!"
—CHRISTOPHER MO[ORE], author of *The Stupidest Angel*

"If you haven't read Mellick you're not nearly perverse enough for the twenty first century."
—JACK KETCHUM, author of *The Girl Next Door*

"Carlton Mellick III is one of bizarro fiction's most talented practitioners, a virtuoso of the surreal, science fictional tale."
—CORY DOCTOROW, author of *Little Brother*

"Bizarre, twisted, and emotionally raw—Carlton Mellick's fiction is the literary equivalent of putting your brain in a blender."
—BRIAN KEENE, author of *The Rising*

"Carlton Mellick III exemplifies the intelligence and wit that lurks between its lurid covers. In a genre where crude titles are an art in themselves, Mellick is a true artist."
—*THE GUARDIAN*

"Just as Pop had Andy Warhol and Dada Tristan Tzara, the bizarro movement has its very own P. T. Barnum-type practitioner. He's the mutton-chopped author of such books as *Electric Jesus Corpse* and *The Menstruating Mall*, the illustrator, editor, and instructor of all things bizarro, and his name is Carlton Mellick III."
—*DETAILS MAGAZINE*

"The most original novelist working today? The most outrageous? The most unpredictable? These aren't easy superlatives to make; however, Carlton Mellick may well be all of those things, behind a canon of books that all irreverently depart from the form and concepts of traditional novels, and adventure the reader into a howling, dark fantasyland of the most bizarre, over-the-top, and mind-warping inventiveness."
—EDWARD LEE, author of *Header*

"Discussing Bizarro literature without mentioning Mellick is like discussing weird-ass muttonchopped authors without mentioning Mellick."
—*CRACKED.COM*

"Carlton is an acquired taste, but he hooks you like a drug."
—HUNTER SHEA, author of *Forest of Shadows*

"Mellick's career is impressive because, despite the fact that he puts out a few books a year, he has managed to bring something new to the table every time… Every Mellick novel is packed with more wildly original concepts than you could find in the current top ten *New York Times* bestsellers put together."
—*VERBICIDE*

"Mellick's guerrilla incursions combine total geekboy fandom and love with genuine, unbridled outsider madness. As such, it borders on genius, in the way only true outsider art can."
—*FANGORIA*

Also by Carlton Mellick III

Satan Burger
Electric Jesus Corpse (Fan Club Exclusive)
Sunset With a Beard (stories)
Razor Wire Pubic Hair
Teeth and Tongue Landscape
The Steel Breakfast Era
The Baby Jesus Butt Plug
Fishy-fleshed
The Menstruating Mall
Ocean of Lard (with Kevin L. Donihe)
Punk Land
Sex and Death in Television Town
Sea of the Patchwork Cats
The Haunted Vagina
Cancer-cute (Fan Club Exclusive)
War Slut
Sausagey Santa
Ugly Heaven
Adolf in Wonderland
Ultra Fuckers
Cybernetrix
The Egg Man
Apeshit
The Faggiest Vampire
The Cannibals of Candyland
Warrior Wolf Women of the Wasteland
The Kobold Wizard's Dildo of Enlightenment +2
Zombies and Shit
Crab Town
The Morbidly Obese Ninja
Barbarian Beast Bitches of the Badlands
Fantastic Orgy (stories)

I Knocked Up Satan's Daughter
Armadillo Fists
The Handsome Squirm
Tumor Fruit
Kill Ball
Cuddly Holocaust
Hammer Wives (stories)
Village of the Mermaids
Quicksand House
Clusterfuck
Hungry Bug
Tick People
Sweet Story
As She Stabbed Me Gently in the Face
ClownFellas: Tales of the Bozo Family
Bio Melt
Every Time We Meet at the Dairy Queen,
Your Whole Fucking Face Explodes
The Terrible Thing That Happens
Exercise Bike
Spider Bunny
The Big Meat
Parasite Milk
Stacking Doll
Neverday
The Boy with the Chainsaw Heart
Mouse Trap
Snuggle Club
The Bad Box
Full Metal Octopus
Goblins on the Other Side
The Girl with the Barbed Wire Hair
You Always Try to Kill Me in Your Dreams
Glass Children
Why I Married a Clown Girl From the Dimension of Death

APESHIP

CARLTON MELLICK III

ERASERHEAD PRESS
PORTLAND, OREGON

ERASERHEAD PRESS
205 NE BRYANT
PORTLAND, OR 97211

WWW.ERASERHEADPRESS.COM

ISBN: 978-1-62105-109-1

Copyright © 2024 by Carlton Mellick III

Cover art copyright © 2024 Anton Vilkin

All rights reserved. No part of this book may be reproduced or transmitted in any form or by any means, electronic or mechanical, including photocopying, recording, or by any information storage and retrieval system, without the written consent of the publisher, except where permitted by law.

Printed in the USA.

AUTHOR'S NOTE

Apeship is the first book that I wrote in my new house. This makes it an extra special one for me. I never thought I'd ever be able to afford a house as a full time writer. For those who don't know, the typical income of a really, really successful novelist is a little less than that of a part time fast food worker. But I managed to buy one, even during the overpriced housing market of the past few years. There are two reasons why I was able to accomplish this seemingly impossible task: First, I decided to move out of Portland (where the median cost of a house is 800k) and go to the Grays Harbor area on the Washington Coast where houses are a third the price. Second, my book *The Haunted Vagina* had gone viral so many times during the pandemic that I was able to save up a thirty percent down payment. Now I have a house. It's nearly a hundred years old and in a flood zone, but I have a house. I call it *The House That The Haunted Vagina Built*. Perhaps one day I will come up with an even stupider idea of a book and pay the house off or buy a bigger one. Time will tell.

In any case, I was in such a good mood after the move that I decided to write the book everyone has been asking me to write for the past decade: another sequel to *Apeshit*. Like the other sequel, *Clusterfuck*, this book stands on its own and you don't need to have read the first one to follow the story. I hope you enjoy it as much as the previous two.

—Carlton Mellick III   8/22/2023 8:46am

CHAPTER ONE
LILY

Lily is a weird little kid.

    She's the cutest, most popular girl in the seventh grade, but there's something off about her. Maybe it's because she was raised by a narcissistic bitch of a mother and a self-absorbed douche of a father, who both treated her like a lifeless glass ornament whose only purpose was to show off her adorable looks to their rich friends. She was forced to win beauty pageants since she was five and take ballet lessons until her toes were bruised and swollen. She was forced to put her hair in pigtails and dress in clothes that made her look half her age because her mother didn't want people to think she was old for having a daughter who's practically a teenager. She was given all the toys and money and possessions she could possibly want, as long as she didn't ask to be loved.

    Lily's parents didn't love anyone but themselves. They didn't have it in them to love anyone else, not even their own daughter. And because of this Lily is growing into a weird, spoiled sociopath who doesn't connect well to other human beings.

    She sees other kids at school as objects to torture and make fun of. She doesn't have any real friends. She doesn't even understand the purpose of having friends. She's surely going to grow up to be an absolute monster and her parents have no idea just what kind of psychopath they've created.

The only thing Lily's father can tell that's wrong with her is the way she plays with dead animals she finds in the woods on his property. She likes to bring dead bunnies and birds and squirrels into the house and dress them up in doll clothes. She hides them in her closet and under her bed. She plays with the rotting animals like Barbie dolls and has entire backstories for each of them, like Roger the dead skunk butler with a gambling addiction and Jessica the prim and proper dead pigeon housemaid who speaks with a Portuguese accent. They are more important to her than the most expensive toys she receives at Christmas time. But even more disturbing is that the smell doesn't seem to bother her. She won't even burn the scented candles her mom sets up around her room.

At first, Lily's parents thought that she was obsessed with dead things. But it's not death that interests her. Lily just has a fascination with raw meat. She likes the way it feels in her fingers. She spends hours in the kitchen, rubbing her fingernails on raw chicken breasts and squishing them against the palms of her hands. She loves the sensation of a cold sirloin steak on her cheek or chicken wings tangled in her hair. The texture is pleasant to her. The smell is sweet like flowers. She wishes she could take a bath in raw meat and rub the oils all over her body.

And lately, she's been especially interested in raw hamburger meat. Her parents never allow ground beef in the house because her mom calls it junk food that makes women fat. So Lily has been buying it in secret, using her allowance. She plays with the ground meat like playdough, sculpting it into strange shapes, molding it into grotesque works of art.

Even now, on the way to the docks, Lily has a clump of hamburger meat in her pocket, squishing her fingers into it the whole ride there. Her father is at the wheel, driving his vintage Mercedes with the top down, blasting Fine Young Cannibals so loud that it disturbs all the other drivers on the road.

"Are you excited to spend a weekend with Daddy Cool?" her father asks, looking down at her with a stupid smug smile on his face.

The girl just shrugs and continues squishing the hamburger meat between her fingers.

Lily hates every single member of her family. She hates her bratty little brothers who always steal her underwear and draw poop in the crotches with brown crayon. She hates her narcissistic snob of a mother who criticizes every little thing she does from chewing her fingernails to breathing improperly. But the person she hates more than anyone is her father, Blaise. Partially because he's a self-absorbed douche who thinks he's god's gift to the world, but also because he insists on being called by his self-given nickname: Daddy Cool.

Her father lowers his 1989 designer sunglasses on his forehead. "Daddy Cool's going to show you a good time this weekend. Guaranteed. Just wait until you see my new boat. It's a thing of beauty. Daddy Cool rides in style."

He holds up his hand in the shape of a sailboat and moves it across her face like it's sailing through ocean waves, making whooshing noises with his pursed lips.

Lily can't handle his whole Daddy Cool shtick, especially when he talks about himself in the third person. Whenever he takes the family on a vacation or out to a fancy restaurant, he forces everyone to refer to him as Daddy Cool in order to show appreciation. Feeding his ego is how he expects his family to repay him for all the money he spends on them.

He'll say, "Daddy who?"

And everyone in the family will have to respond, "Daddy Cooool!"

It's beyond embarrassing to Lily and her mother, especially when it causes a scene, disturbing everyone else around them. But Lily's younger brothers seem to love calling their father Daddy Cool. The twins are only in the first grade and haven't yet realized what a huge douche their father really is. They eat it up and he can't get enough of the attention.

"Daddy who?" her father will ask only two minutes later.

Her brothers have been trained to react on command, like

obedient little puppies. "Daddy Cooool!"

"That's right," he'll say, nodding his head with a stupid satisfied smile on his face. "And don't you forget it."

But even worse than that is the time she heard her father lean over to her mother after an especially expensive dinner on a family vacation and whisper to her, "Let's ditch the kids and go back to our room. Daddy Cool's getting his dick sucked tonight."

And those words have been scarred into her brain forever.

⚓

Lily's father gets frustrated by his daughter's lack of enthusiasm to see his new yacht. No matter how much he tries to put her in a happy mood, she won't stop being a miserable pain in the butt. She hasn't even called him Daddy Cool once and it's getting on his nerves. He would have brought the twins instead of her if they weren't too young to go out on the boat. At least they still understand just how cool of a dad he is.

"Come on, baby girl," her father says, turning down the music. "You've never been on a boating trip with me before. You have to be at least a little excited."

Lily shrugs again.

"You're going to love it I promise," he says. "There's nothing like being out on the wide-open sea. It's beautiful. Maybe we'll even see a mermaid. You like mermaids, don't you?"

"No," Lily says.

"What?" he says, shocked by her response. "All girls like mermaids."

"Mermaids are retarded."

"Hey!" he yells at her, pulling over on the side of the road. He looks her in the eyes. "Don't say *retarded*. It's offensive."

Lily shrugs. "Fine."

"Fine *what?*" he asks.

"Fine, I won't say retarded. Are you happy?"

"That's better," he says. Then he gets back on the road and they continue on their way. "It makes me sick when people say retarded. Did you know your cousin Dean was retarded?"

Lily looks at him with a confused face. "No, he's not. He's just stupid."

"Well, he seemed retarded to me."

Lily shakes her head and ignores him again. Her dad is the biggest asshole she's ever met. Not only does he get mad at her for using the R-word, even though he uses it more than anyone she's ever met, he also criticizes his own nephew even though he is missing and presumed dead. Dean, who liked to go by the name Extreme Dean, went missing last fall after he went caving with some friends from his fraternity. The dumbass probably died in a cave and her dad doesn't care one bit. It's not that she cares either, but she knows better than to say bad things about the dead. Her aunt, Dean's mom, is the only person in their family who has ever been remotely nice to her and she can at least sympathize with the woman for losing her son. She's the only one who lets her play with hamburger meat without being judged or yelled at.

Lily stews for a while. She can't believe she was forced to go on a boating trip with her dad. It's probably because her parents are getting a divorce and her father doesn't want her to side with her mother. He's trying to earn some points. It's not that he loves his daughter so much that he can't let her go. He just can't handle the blow to his ego if any of his children chose his wife over him. He's the cool, fun parent. He's Daddy Cool. There's no way he's going to lose to that stuck-up bitch.

"You're going to love Rachel," her father says. "She's a cool chick. Way cooler than your mom. And she's smoking hot. Goddamn she's fine." Her father pumps his fist and grunts, humping his pelvis toward his steering wheel. "Man, I love that girl."

Lily rolls her eyes, completely disgusted with her father. He's been dating Rachel for the past four years behind her mother's back. She's some college girl who's only ten years older than Lily yet twenty-five years younger than her father. It's disturbing to Lily that her father actually wants the three of them to go on a vacation together. Lily knows she's going to hate her. No worthwhile human being could ever possibly want to be with her father for that long unless they were just as intolerable as he is. And facing three days stuck on a boat in the middle of the ocean with both of them is probably going to be the most difficult thing Lily's ever had to endure.

⚓

When they get to the docks, Lily's father can't help his excitement. His eyes are wide and his fingers are squeezing into fists. Lily's never seen such a childish amount of enthusiasm coming from her dad before.

"Are you ready?" he asks her.

Lily shrugs.

He leans in closer. "Daddy who?"

He winks.

"Huh?" Lily asks with an annoyed expression.

He says, "Come on. Say it."

Then he asks again, "Daddy who?"

"I'm not going to say it," she tells him.

The smile falls from his face. His enthusiasm turns to frustration.

"It's Daddy Cool," he tells her. "Say Daddy Cool."

She groans at him. "Why do you need me to call you that? It's so cringey."

His face becomes more serious. "Don't fuck this up for me. I need you to do this one thing. It's important."

Lily rolls her eyes. "Fine…"

The smile returns to his face. "Daddy Who?"

"Daddy Cool…" she says in the most apathetic tone possible.

"And don't you forget it!" he yells, hopping out of his convertible without opening the door. "Daddy Cool coming aboard!"

Lily's soul dies a little.

They get their luggage and head toward the dock where three college-aged students are hanging out, drinking Bud Light Cheladas and sharing a joint. There's a bitchy-looking girl in a crop top and jean shorts, a tan shirtless guy who looks like he's from the cast of Jersey Shore, and a timid-looking girl in a flowery sundress.

"There they are." Her father waves at them with a smug smile on his face. "Let's go say hi."

Lily lets out a long sigh and puts her fingers back into her pocket, hoping a handful of hamburger meat will send a wave of relaxation through her body.

⚓

"Here they come," Rachel says to the others while tugging up her crop top.

The guy with no shirt tosses the joint on the ground and stomps it out before the young girl can see. "We're really going out on a boat with that prick?"

"It's just one more weekend and I can finally be done with him," she says.

"Why don't you just break it off with him right now and get it over with?"

"He said he'd buy me a car when we get back," Rachel says. "I don't mind fucking him for another weekend if it means getting a new car."

Blaise is Rachel's sugar daddy. He's been paying her rent for the past four years, paying her college tuition, paying off her credit cards every month, and buying her pretty much anything she wants whenever they're together. All she has to do is sleep with him once or twice a week. It's been a favorable relationship, but it's about time it came to an end. Rachel just graduated and doesn't need his tuition money anymore. She can finally get a good job and support herself. And now that Blaise is getting a divorce from his wife he's going to be free to spend more time with her. He'll probably ask her to move in with him. And there's only so much time she can spend with Blaise Brockman without wanting to rip her hair out. One more weekend and she can get her car and then break things off with him for good.

As Blaise comes closer, he stretches out his arms and yells, "Daddy who?"

"Daddy Cool!" Rachel yells, then fake-laughs, feigning excitement to see her douchebag sugar daddy.

"Did you just call him Daddy Cool?" the shirtless guy asks, quiet enough that Blaise doesn't hear him.

"Just go with it," Rachel says.

She runs toward Blaise and jumps into his arms, hugging him tight and kissing him on the cheek.

⚓

Lily can't believe that her father's girlfriend also calls him Daddy Cool. It's probably the worst thing that could have ever happened to her. She really doesn't want to be alive anymore.

"I think I threw up in my mouth a little," she tells her dad and girlfriend, but they don't hear her comment.

When they finish their embrace, they both look over at the girl.

"Rachel, this is my daughter, Lily," he tells his girlfriend. Then he turns to his daughter. "Lily, this is Rachel, the woman I've been telling you about."

Rachel holds out her hand and says, "Nice to meet you, Lily."

Lily eyeballs the woman for a moment, examining her up and down. Rachel has dark red lipstick and thick black eye makeup, witchy pale skin, and short curly brown hair that dances in the ocean breeze. Lily can't believe her father is actually dating the woman. She's so much younger and more attractive than he is. Not as attractive as her mother when she was young, but definitely more attractive than she is now despite her trashy, whorish style. It's no wonder why her parents are getting divorced.

"Hi," Lily says, shaking the woman's hand. She uses the hand that was in her pocket full of raw hamburger meat.

The look of confusion on Rachel's face when she notices all the meat grease on her palms and fingers is priceless to Lily. Rachel doesn't say anything about it. She just turns around and wipes the grease on the side of her shorts, wondering where the hell it came from.

Rachel leads them to the other two and introduces them.

She points at the shirtless guy and says, "This is my brother, Conner." Then she points to the girl in the flowery dress. "And this is my best friend in the world, Addy."

Blaise goes to them and says, "Hi, I'm Blaise. But you can call me Daddy Cool."

"Daddy Cool?" Conner says, putting on his friendliest face for his sister's sake. "Sweet. You can call me Con, bro."

"Con Bro?" Blaise asks, nodding in approval. "Daddy Cool and Con Bro. I think we'll get along just fine."

Conner laughs and says, "Sure. Whatever, man."

Blaise goes in and gives him a high five. The college guy just goes with it and steps away. When Blaise approaches the other girl, she doesn't want to have anything to do with him. But he forces an awkwardly long hug on the poor girl.

"Nice to meet you, Addy," he says. "I've heard all about you."

Addy tries to pull away from him, saying, "It's nice to meet you, too, Daddy Cool."

Lily makes eye contact with Addy and says, "Please don't call him Daddy Cool."

When Blaise hears his daughter, he turns to her and pulls her forward, "And this is Lily. She'll be coming along with us this weekend. Don't worry about her age. She can hang. A little weird, but she's cool."

Lily just frowns and waves at the young adults. "Hi."

They nod their heads and turn away, trying to pretend she doesn't exist.

"Are you ready to go?" Blaise asks the group.

They all nod.

Blaise picks up his stuff. "Then let's go get Daddy Cool's dick wet."

And he heads off toward the boats.

After Rachel's friends look at her, wondering what the hell is wrong with that prick, she explains, "He calls his boat his dick."

Conner and Addy look at each other and say, "Ohhh… Gross."

⚓

Although Blaise calls his yacht his dick, the actual name of the boat is even more disgusting.

"*The Crotch Moistener?*" Rachel asks Blaise when she sees the side of the ship. "You actually called your boat *The Crotch Moistener?*"

Blaise is stoked on the name. He nods his head with pride. "Damn right. Have you ever seen anything that makes you more wet than the sight of this boat?"

The ship stands out among all the other boats in the marina. It looks like it was designed by Italian sports car engineers, with a sleek exterior and an almost futuristic style. Rachel knew it was going to be big and ostentatious, but she had no idea just how fancy it was going to be. Blaise has money but he's not a billionaire. He must have drained his savings and cashed out a ton of investments in order to pay for it.

"It's nice," Rachel says, ignoring his question. "Must have been expensive."

"Ten times your college education," he tells her. "Best thing I ever bought."

Conner comes up behind them, nodding his head. "Sweet boat, bro."

"Yeah, I really like it, Mr. Brockman," Addy says.

Blaise looks over at Addy and raises his sunglasses. "Please, Mr. Brockman was my father's name. Call me Daddy Cool."

"Can I just call you Blaise?" she asks.

He lowers his sunglasses and turns away from her. "No."

And then they board the ship.

⚓

The college kids freak out when they see the sundeck of the ship. It's the most luxurious thing any of them have ever seen, like the patio of a swanky bar. They drop all of their luggage by their feet and take a look around.

All of them are impressed beyond words, including Blaise. Even though it is his boat, he is unapologetically impressed with himself at all times for all reasons. The only one who is not impressed is Lily, who is so young and has been raised in such a luxurious lifestyle that it takes a lot more than this to make an impact on her.

The two girls run across the deck, examining every detail.

"Oh my god, this is so amazing!" Rachel cries. "This has got to be the nicest ship in the harbor!" She really lays the compliments on thick and her boyfriend eats it up. She knows the only reason he invited her and her friends on this trip is because he's desperate for praise and admiration. Blaise is the kind of person who thrives on being appreciated and will always spend any amount of money on you as long as he gets the attention he desires. Rachel has learned this lesson well and has spent the last four years of her life using it to her advantage. No matter how big of a selfish douche her sugar daddy is, she knows exactly how and when to push his money buttons.

Conner goes over to Blaise and nods his head at the rich guy. "Nice going, bro. This is bigger than my whole apartment."

Blaise snickers. "This is bigger than five of your apartments."

Conner was just trying to be nice, but can't help but feel insulted. Blaise doesn't even realize that his apartment is actually pretty nice. It's an 1800 square feet four bedroom that costs thirty-five hundred a month. He has three roommates, but still. The boat isn't even twice the size of his apartment, let alone five times. He knows Blaise is some big shot hedge fund asshole but he doesn't appreciate being talked down to. He lets it slide for his sister's sake, but if the prick doesn't watch his step Conner might end up laying him out on the deck of his own ship.

"Let me show you the bridge," Blaise tells him.

Conner agrees to let it go and follows him.

"This ship has muscle, I tell you," Blaise says. "It's got two twin-turbocharged V12 engines with a max speed of thirty knots. The thing is a goddamned Lamborghini of the sea."

Conner feigns interest. "Sweet, bro."

"You're really going to appreciate this. Maybe I'll even let you drive for a while."

Lily follows after them because she doesn't want to be alone with her father's girlfriend. She can tell that the shirtless guy dislikes her father as much as anyone who meets him, but her dad has a desperate need to come across as manly to other men. He loves being showered with praise by women, but seeks the approval of other men. Even one who's half his age, the kind of guy who would've bullied him when he was younger.

But when they get to the cockpit, there's already somebody there. An older Hispanic man who is investigating the controls and testing the equipment.

When Blaise sees him, he freaks the fuck out.

"Who the hell are you?" her father cries. "What are you doing on my ship?"

The man isn't fazed by her father's outrage and says, "Ahh, Mr. Brockman. I didn't realize you came aboard."

"This is private property," Blaise says. "You're trespassing."

The man ignores his words and says, "I'm Pablo Ramirez. Mr. Richards wasn't able to make it due to a medical emergency. I'll be taking over for him."

"Like hell you are," Blaise yells. "I didn't ask for you. I asked for Tom."

Pablo seems confused by his outrage. "As I said, Mr. Richards couldn't make it."

"I don't care!" Blaise yells. "Get the fuck off my ship."

The man looks dumbfounded by his response. He leaves the bridge and goes toward the sundeck.

"I'm sorry, Mr. Brockman. We didn't realize this would be a problem."

"You didn't steal anything, did you?" Blaise yells. "Empty your pockets."

The three college kids are shocked by the middle-aged man's response. They gather around them.

"What's the problem?" Addy asks.

Lily turns to her and says, "My dad's super racist."

Blaise gets offended at his daughter's words. Everyone, including Pablo, heard her.

"I'm not racist!" Blaise cries. "I just don't trust anyone but Tom with my ship."

Pablo pleads with him, "I assure you I'm every bit as qualified as Mr. Richards."

Blaise shakes his head. "I'm sorry, pal. But I don't know you. Get off my boat. I'll pilot this thing myself."

Rachel looks worried. "Are you sure? Do you even know how to drive a boat?"

"Of course I do!" he cries. "I wouldn't have bought this thing otherwise."

Then he glares at Pablo and says, "Go on. Get out of here."

"But there's issues I've found with…" Pablo begins.

"I don't care! Get off my boat or I'm calling the police." Blaise takes out his cell phone and dials 911.

"Okay, fine," Pablo says. "I'm going, but if you just listen to me for a second—"

Blaise interrupts him once he gets through to 911.

"Hello?" he says into the phone. "Get me the police. There's a Mexican trying to steal my boat."

"Jesus Christ, Karen," Conner says, too quiet for Blaise to hear.

Pablo holds out his hands as he leaves the ship. "Okay, I'm going."

Once he's on the dock, Blaise apologizes to the 911 operator and puts his phone away.

"Fucking asshole," he says. "I can't believe Tom would do this to me."

Rachel says, "What are we going to do now? Should we cancel the trip?"

Blaise shakes his head. "Hell no. I can drive this ship just fine. I only hired Tom so that I'd have more free time, but I can do it myself."

"Are you sure?" Rachel asks.

"Of course I'm sure," Blaise says. "It's my boat. I don't need a *Pablo* getting us lost at sea."

The college kids groan quietly.

"You know Rachel and I are half Puerto Rican, right?" Conner says to Blaise.

"Shut the fuck up, dude!" Rachel yells at her brother, punching him in the shoulder.

Blaise either doesn't hear them or chooses not to. He turns back to the group and says, "Don't worry about it. Just a minor setback. Let's just head out to sea and have a good time."

He heads for the bridge.

Conner turns to his sister and says, "Are you sure this is a good idea?"

Rachel shrugs. "I'm sure it will be fine."

But all of them, especially Lily, think that leaving Blaise in charge of their safety is a very bad idea.

⚓

Once they're out on the open seas with the land far behind them, the group decides to relax and have a good time. Blaise puts the boat on autopilot and heads back to the deck.

"Who wants a drink?" Blaise asks the group.

Conner holds up a warm can of clamato beer and says, "Way ahead of you, bro."

Blaise scoffs at the college boy and says, "I'll make you a *real* drink. Do you like scotch?"

Conner shrugs. "Scotch? Sure."

Blaise pours four glasses of Johnny Walker Blue on the rocks and hands one to Conner.

"This is 200 dollars a bottle scotch," Blaise says with a smug smile on his face.

"Oh, sweet," Conner says. "Thanks, bro."

Conner takes a large swig, swallowing without savoring it.

"Smooth," Conner nods with approval. "I once tried a 500 dollar bottle of scotch. It was amazing. This is good, too."

Blaise frowns at him, annoyed that he didn't blow his mind in the way that he thought he would. He turns to his sugar baby.

"Want a drinkipoo, babe?" he asks Rachel, calling her over.

Her eyes light up in excitement and she goes to him, taking the drink from his hand. When she tastes it, she says, "Oh my god, this is good stuff. I think it's the best liquor I've ever had."

Lily can't handle how fake the girl is. Rachel obviously doesn't like the drink and would've preferred something lighter, but seems to know all too well that telling the truth to Daddy

Cool is a fast path to conflict. Lily can't stand people who do that with her father.

"Damn right it is," Blaise says, reaching his hand around Rachel's waist and pulling her closer.

"You always have the best liquor," she says, giggling.

Blaise smiles. "Daddy who?"

She rolls her eyes in a flirtatious way. "Daddy Cool."

Then he kisses her on the cheek.

Lily rolls her eyes and goes to sit on a chair nearby. She plays a game on her cell phone while the battery still lasts, trying to block out all of the people around her. It's not even been an hour and she already wishes she was back home.

"Did you bring the outfit I sent you?" Blaise asks Rachel.

She thinks about it for a second. "Uhhh... the bathing suit?"

"Yeah, isn't it perfect?" he asks.

Rachel takes another sip of her drink and swallows with a loud gulp. "Yeah, I love it."

"Why don't you put it on then?" He squeezes her hip.

"Right now?" she asks.

"Yeah."

"Are we going swimming?" she asks.

Blaise gets annoyed with her. "This is a yacht. It should be filled with hot babes in bathing suits at all times. It doesn't matter if we're going swimming or not."

Rachel takes another large swig of her scotch and puts it down. "Sure, I'll go put it on."

She grabs her luggage and heads below deck.

Blaise calls out. "It's the room on the end. The big one."

She waves him off and heads downstairs.

When he makes eye contact with Addy, he tells her, "Do you have a bathing suit?"

Addy shrugs.

"The weather's nice. Perfect bikini weather."

"I'm good," Addy says.

Blaise nods his head and finishes his scotch. Then he looks over at Conner who is messing around with his phone, his legs up on a table, ignoring everyone around him.

"Make yourselves comfortable," Blaise says.

Then he goes back to the bar to pour some more drinks.

⚓

When Rachel comes out, she's wearing a G-string bikini designed to look like a sailor outfit. It's more fetish cosplay than bathing suit, with a white and blue collar, tiny black bow on her chest, and a sailor's hat on her head.

"Holy shit, babe!" Blaise cries out when he sees her. "That's so hot!"

She poses for him, showing off the outfit that he bought her, but she dares not turn around. With her pale bare ass showing, she can't help but feel embarrassed around her brother and best friend, not to mention her boyfriend's twelve-year-old daughter.

"That's the outfit you wear on a yacht!" Blaise yells.

He goes to high-five Conner, but then realizes the guy is her brother and lowers his hand, pretending it never happened.

Then he rushes to Rachel and wraps his arms around her, "You look great, babe. Daddy Cool's getting a coolito."

Nobody wants to know what a coolito is.

"Oh, I'll join you," Blaise says. "I got my own outfit for this occasion."

He goes to his luggage and digs out a captain's hat, then puts it on his head.

"See," Blaise says, pointing at his hat. "The captain's on deck."

Nobody is impressed. Rachel looks at him, kind of annoyed that he only has to wear a hat instead of the ridiculous outfit he forced her to put on. But she goes with it and pretends that he's the sexiest man she's ever seen.

"That's pretty hot," she says, pressing herself against him. "I guess we're going to have to call you Captain Cool now."

The smile falls off his face when she says this and he pushes her back. "No, it's Daddy Cool." He takes off the hat and throws it on the table, startling Lily and Conner who were absorbed on their phones. "Just Daddy Cool."

And then he storms off to the bridge of the ship.

"Jesus Christ," Addy says. "What's wrong with that guy?"

Then she notices that she's talking shit about Lily's father in front of the girl and apologizes.

Lily ignores her and says, "He has a small penis."

Then the college kids break out into laughter. They pat her on the shoulders and cheer her on.

"I like this kid," Conner says.

"She must take after her mom," Rachel says.

But when she hears Rachel praising her, Lily hides her face in her phone. She doesn't want to be liked by this woman, especially not for criticizing her shithead father. And bringing up her mother is even more irritating. Lily's mother is the most intolerable woman on the planet and the last person she'd ever want to be compared to. She wishes they'd all jump off the side of the ship and leave her in peace.

⚓

Lily decides to do her own thing for a while. She's had enough of her father and the college students. She brings her luggage below deck and pulls out large freezer bags of ground beef that fill an entire suitcase, about twenty pounds of meat. She puts half away in the refrigerator and takes the rest out onto the kitchen counter. She lets out a long sigh as she digs her hands into the pile of meat, squishing her fingers deep inside. The meat has just barely defrosted so it's cold to the touch. She warms it with her body heat, then sculpts it into a castle.

It's been a long time since Lily has built a sandcastle, but it was something she loved to do when she was younger. Her parents took her to beaches all over the Caribbean and Hawaii and Thailand, so she's had plenty of practice building castles in the sand. But she likes building them with hamburger even more. The ease at which she can sculpt the meat and form it into exactly what she wants is satisfying to her. She especially likes the texture and smell of the raw meat. She enjoys how it feels between her fingers.

It doesn't take long until the meat is a tall tower with windows and balconies and a moat of grease around the outside. Lily's hands are covered in red chunks and foamy white fat. She licks her fingers, wetting them to make it easier to sculpt. The flavor is tangy and pleasant. It's the only moment she's had all day to herself and she wishes she could spend the entire trip doing this. She hopes the others are too distracted to pay attention to her. Nothing would make her happier than spending all three days alone with her meat.

But it doesn't take long before her father comes to check up on her. She's in the middle of taking pictures of her creation on her phone when Blaise walks in and freaks out over the mess.

"What the hell are you doing in here?" he yells.

Lily groans and rolls her eyes. "I'm sculpting."

"Are you fucking crazy?" he asks. "Where the hell did you get all of this meat?"

"I brought it," she explains, pointing at the greasy freezer bags on the floor.

Blaise wants to smash the meat sculpture in anger, but the idea of getting any of it on his hands grosses him out.

"This is disgusting," he says. "What would Rachel think of you if she saw this? Do you want her to think you're a weirdo?"

Lily shrugs. "I don't care what she thinks."

He gets the garbage bags from under the sink and puts the box on the counter next to her. "Just clean this shit up and come outside. I have an important announcement to make."

⚓

When Lily comes out, the others are all standing around with drinks in their hands, pretending to laugh at Blaise's stupid jokes.

"Finally, you're here," Blaise says to Lily as she comes out, annoyed with how long she took even though it was his fault for making her clean up the hamburger meat in the kitchen.

Blaise gathers everyone around him and says, "I have something important I wanted you all here for."

Lily comes in close and the four of them gather around her father, not sure why it's so important.

Blaise turns to Rachel and looks deep into her eyes. He says, "Babe, these last four years with you have been the happiest I've been in a long time. You're the best thing in Daddy Cool's life and I want you to know that."

As he says this, Rachel's jaw drops open and she steps back a little. She says, "Oh shit..."

"I invited the most important people in your life on this trip, and the most important person in my life," he looks over at Lily and gives her a wink, then turns back to Rachel, "because I wanted you all to witness this occasion. "

Everyone but Blaise notices the panic filling Rachel's eyes.

Blaise continues, "Now that I'm divorcing my bitch of a wife, I'm finally able to commit myself to the only woman who really appreciates me."

"Don't you fucking dare," Lily says.

Her father ignores her. He pulls a ring out of his pocket and gets on one knee.

Then he asks her, "Rachel, will you make Daddy Cool the happiest, coolest dad on the planet? Will you marry me?"

The group goes quiet. Rachel puts her hands in her face, hiding her reaction. She knew that it was going to be a problem now that her sugar daddy was leaving his wife, but she had no idea that he would actually propose to her. It's almost like he wants to lock it down now that she's graduated from college. Without him paying her tuition, she doesn't really have a need for him anymore. The prospect of marrying a rich guy and living in luxury for the rest of your life might be appealing to a lot of women in her position, but she didn't go to college for nothing. She has things she wants to do with her life. Becoming a trophy wife to an intolerable douchebag like Blaise has zero appeal to her whatsoever. And everyone but Blaise understands this before she even has to say a word.

Rachel just stands there for a while, leaving the group in silence. She turns away and takes a large swig of her drink. Then she clears her throat.

Blaise's smile falls from his face, confused about why she would take so long to respond. He expected her to be over the moon with excitement. This entire trip revolves around her being overwhelmed with happiness over the idea of becoming his bride. But Rachel looks like she's about to be sick.

"What's wrong?" Blaise asks. "Is your mind blown or what?"

"Umm…" Rachel tries to smile as she turns back to him. "This is pretty sudden."

"Sudden?" Blaise gets annoyed. "We've been together for four years."

"Yeah, but it's not like we've been dating," she says. "We had an agreement. I slept with you whenever you wanted in exchange for paying for my school and apartment."

A look of shock fills Blaise's face. "Yeah, maybe at first, but we grew past that, didn't we? I thought we were really an item. Daddy Cool and Baby Cool. We're great for each other."

Rachel shrugs. "Yeah, sure. It was fun having a guy with a lot of money buy me anything I wanted, but you knew we weren't serious, right?" Then she lets out a laugh. "I mean you're like fifty or something. I'm twenty-two. I'm not ready to settle down with anyone."

Blaise is obviously crushed. His face is turning red. Tears

pool in the corners of his eyes. He's never been more humiliated in his life.

"Fine, I get it," Blaise says, standing up and putting the ring back in his pocket. "I've only spent more money on you than I have my own children."

Rachel realizes that she's just destroyed the guy's massive ego and tries to make it right. She goes to him and puts her hands on his shoulders. "Come on, don't be upset. The last thing I wanted to do is hurt you. You're my Daddy Cool."

He pushes her off of him. She's obviously just trying to stay on his good side so that he still buys her the car he promised.

"If I'm really your Daddy Cool then how could you do this to me?" he asks her. "Do you know how many women would kill to be in your shoes?"

Rachel can't help but laugh at his words. "Yeah, I'm sure there's a lot of women who would love to get their hands on your money."

He doesn't allow her comment to register with him, refusing to acknowledge the absurd idea that his money is the only thing about him that women would find desirable. He thinks he's in decent shape. He thinks he's fun to be around. And even though he's almost fifty years old, he believes that everyone around him would easily take him for a thirty-year-old or even a guy in his late twenties. Nothing that Rachel is saying makes sense to him.

He says, "I only brought you on my yacht and proposed to you because I thought it would make you happy. What the fuck's wrong with you?"

Rachel apologizes and says, "Can we just put this behind us? It's not the end of the world."

She goes to him and wraps her arms around him. He doesn't resist this time, letting her press her half naked body around him. Lily cringes in disgust as she sees the girl's bare ass showing as she hugs her father in the G-string bikini.

"It'll be fine, babe," Rachel says. "Just because I don't want to marry you doesn't mean I don't want to be with you."

The others wonder how many times Rachel has to calm him down like this. He seems like the kind of guy who gets upset a lot. She's not just his sugar baby, she probably also has to act like his therapist. Even Lily sees him as the biggest spoiled brat on the ship despite being the oldest of them.

Blaise hugs her back and says, "You still want to be my Baby Cool?"

Rachel laughs. "Of course."

Blaise pulls back and wipes the tears from his eyes. He nods his head and says, "Daddy Cool understands. You just graduated. You need time. It's okay. I can wait." Then he steps away from her. "But I won't wait forever."

And he goes back to the bridge of the ship, bringing the bottle of scotch with him.

⚓

After he leaves, the others have no idea how to process what just happened. All of them are feeling pretty awkward, especially Lily who is stuck with the college kids while her father is off moping by himself.

"That was fucking insane," Conner says, pulling out a joint and lighting it. "I can't believe he actually did that."

"I know," Addy says. "I nearly shit my pants!"

Rachel just laughs with them and shakes her head. "I did not see that coming. Not for a second."

She snatches the joint from Conner and takes a drag.

"It all makes sense now," Conner says. "He probably knew you were going to dump him when you graduated and thought he'd impress you with this yacht trip. He wanted to show you what you can have if you stuck with him."

"Like this is enough to impress me," Rachel says.

Addy takes the joint and inhales, holding it for a second.

After she exhales, she says, "Are you sure you don't want to change your mind? He *is* pretty loaded."

"Yeah, you can have his Daddy Cool babies!" Conner yells.

"Ewww!" Rachel cries. "That would be so fucking gross!"

The college kids don't seem to care that they're saying all this shit about Lily's father when she's sitting right next to them. She doesn't have a problem with them saying bad things about her father. She thinks of him just as negatively as they do. She's just glad that Rachel didn't agree to marry him. The last thing she wanted to have to deal with is a new stepmother like her.

"You can be Baby Cool forever!" Conner says.

"Fuck that," Rachel says.

Conner won't let it go. "Come on, Baby Cool. You know you want him."

Rachel pushes him. "Don't you *ever* fucking call me that!"

"Oh, we're *always* going to call you that now," Addy says. "It's permanent."

Then the three of them break into laughter.

Lily can't help herself. She decides to speak up.

"You shouldn't make fun of my dad," she tells them.

They go quiet for a moment, only now realizing that the daughter of the guy they were ridiculing was sitting there with them the whole time. Conner and Addy won't even look at her, just sharing the joint and keeping their opinions to themselves.

Only Rachel responds. "I'm sorry, Lily," she tells the girl. "I didn't mean to make fun of your father in front of you. That was rude of us."

Lily shakes her head. "I don't give a fuck about that. I hate my father. I'm just warning you that you shouldn't make fun of him. He freaks out when people make fun of him."

Rachel shrugs. "So what? He's an adult. He can deal with it."

Lily gives her a serious look. "We're out in the middle of

the ocean and he's the only one who can bring us back to land. You don't want to piss him off."

The college kids look at each other and laugh nervously, as though they think the girl is just messing with them.

"What's he going to do?" Conner asks. "Kick us overboard?"

"He kicked my mother out of a moving car on the freeway when she insulted his haircut. She still has the scars."

After she says this, the smiles fall from their faces.

"He can't handle being humiliated by anyone," Lily continues. "You can ignore him. You can annoy him. You can be a bitch to him. Just don't make him feel like a loser. He wouldn't hesitate to set his own ship on fire and take off in the lifeboat rather than let anyone get away with making fun of him like you were doing. That's just the kind of asshole he is."

Lily gets up and heads below deck.

Once she's out of sight, the others break out into laughter again.

"That kid's so freaky!" Conner yells.

"She's even worse than her dad!" Rachel cries.

But Lily doesn't let their words affect her. She goes back to the kitchen and pulls out another bag of hamburger meat from the fridge.

⚓

Lily sits in her bunk, playing with meat on her lap. It's been a few hours since she's seen anyone else. She can hear the college kids laughing and partying on the deck of the boat. They probably raided her father's liquor cabinet and are getting trashed without him.

But she's more concerned about how her father is taking the rejection. He is headed full speed out into the open sea, probably having downed the entire bottle of scotch. The more he's left on his own, the more pissed off he's going to get. He's probably just stewing about what Rachel said to him, her words spinning around in his head.

Lily goes to check on him but the door to the cockpit is locked. She can hear her father in there yelling and cursing in a barely intelligible way.

"Hey, Dad?" she asks, knocking on the door. "Are you okay in there?"

But he doesn't respond, spouting nonsense to no one in particular. He's obviously in bad shape. He doesn't even hear her voice no matter how loudly she calls out to him.

"Maybe we should just go back home," she says.

No response.

Lily heads back down to her bunk, but doesn't feel very safe in her current situation. She thought this trip was going to be boring and annoying, but it's starting to turn into a far worse experience than she imagined. She hopes her father is able to calm down. She hopes he doesn't do anything crazy. But knowing him, he's likely to drive the whole lot of them right into the pits of hell.

CHAPTER TWO
RACHEL

⚓

Rachel is happy that her sugar daddy has been leaving her alone with her friends. She really didn't want to go on this trip with him. She hopes he realizes that their relationship isn't going to last for much longer. Even if he doesn't buy her the car she wants, she'll be okay as long as she can be done with him. Because she doesn't love him. She never has. She doesn't even really like guys at all.

The person she loves most in the world is her best friend, Addy. They've known each other since they were kids but it's only been recently that she admitted her feelings. A week before, Rachel told her that she's had a crush on her for the longest time. She didn't know if Addy was actually interested in women. Addy's never had a boyfriend or a girlfriend. She was practically asexual as far as Rachel knew. But Rachel adored her. She loves her cute brown eyes and chiseled features. There's never been anyone she's found more beautiful than the girl who's been by her side for the majority of her life.

When Addy told her that she felt the same way, Rachel couldn't have been happier. It turned out that Addy has had a crush on her for even longer than Rachel did. Neither of them wanted to admit their feelings because their friendship was so important to them that they didn't want to ruin it. But they are both in love with each other. They can't see themselves with anyone else but one another.

After being together for a single week, they've been making love with each other every day. This is the real reason why Rachel wants to break up with Blaise. She can't wait until he's out of her life so she can spend all of her time with her true love. If there's anyone that she would marry it would be Addy. There's no one else that makes her feel the same way. There's no one else who could possibly make her happy.

Once Conner passes out in his seat, Rachel and Addy have the whole deck of the ship to themselves. Blaise has been ignoring everyone all night and his daughter has gone to bed, so there's no one who can get in their way.

Rachel's eyes meet with Addy's and they just stare at each other for a while, saying nothing. Rachel pulls up the top of her bathing suit, exposing her pale breasts that are goosefleshed from the cold ocean breeze. Addy licks her lips at Rachel's erect caramel-colored nipples and then they attack each other.

Addy jumps on top of Rachel and they dig their tongues into each other's mouths, finally able to make love for the first time that day. Rachel can't handle the fact that she's had to be so affectionate with her sugar daddy in her girlfriend's presence. She wants to show Addy that she's the only person for her. She wants to give herself to her completely.

As they pull each other's clothes off, Addy sees something moving beneath Rachel's skin. Small lumps shift and curl through her abdomen.

"They've gotten so big," Addy says, rubbing her fingers up Rachel's body toward her breasts.

"I know." Rachel smiles, admiring the pulsing lumps in her body. "Isn't it hot?"

Addy looks up at her. "Everything about you is hot."

Then they kiss each other, gripping each other's flesh so tightly that it hurts.

⚓

Rachel has a parasite fetish. She doesn't know why, but for as long as she can remember she's loved the idea of being infected by parasites. The idea of living creatures crawling inside her body is the thing that turns her on more than anything. She's given herself tapeworms and ringworms and all manner of easily obtainable parasites that are common in humans, but they were never good enough. They never did what she wanted them to do. She could barely even feel them, as though they weren't even there at all.

That is, until she heard about a new type of parasite. A strange fish was discovered off the shores of Costa Rica with hundreds of slug-like parasites living in its digestive system. What was most intriguing was that the creatures resembled human fetuses. With black ball eyes, gaping mouths, tiny arms, and webbed fingers that helped them crawl through their host's body.

When Rachel heard about them on the parasite fetish message boards, she knew that she had to have them. She spent so much of Blaise's money on her credit cards in order to get a shipment of their eggs on the dark web. And after swallowing them with the proper amount of fish food, Rachel's life has taken a shift for the better. She couldn't be more in love with the sensations in her body.

What she likes about these types of parasites is how they don't just restrict themselves to the digestive system. Once they grow large enough, they infect the muscles. They crawl under your skin and lay eggs in your tissue fibers.

Rachel is in love with the squirming sensation. They don't move around all the time and are most active during the nighttime. Whenever they are at peak shifting, she can't help but get aroused. She wants to bounce on anything that moves.

She's not just turned on by being infected by the parasites.

She also loves the idea of giving them to other people, especially those she dislikes. Blaise probably doesn't even realize he's been infected by them. The last few times they've had sex, Rachel could feel them leaving her body, slithering out of her vaginal canal and into Blaise's urethra. He moaned in pleasure at the sensation, with no idea what it could've been. Rachel can't wait to see how he reacts once the parasites breed and spread out across his body. If they haven't broken up by then she's sure it will be the thing that gets him out of her life forever.

⚓

At this time of night, on the deck of the ship, Rachel's parasites are especially active. They send a ripple of sexual energy across her body. She can't keep her hands off of Addy, pressing her shivering flesh as close to her as possible.

Addy doesn't share the same fetish as Rachel, but she likes the attention that she gets whenever the parasites are squirming. She's turned on by them just because Rachel is turned on. And anything that makes Rachel happy makes her happy.

Rachel looks her girlfriend in the eyes and begs her in a desperate tone, "I need it." She grabs Addy by the back of the neck. "Please."

Addy nods her head and Rachel says, "Come on."

Rachel pulls her girlfriend's head between her legs, and pulls her bikini bottom halfway down to expose her shaved pubic region.

Addy doesn't hesitate. She extends her tongue and presses it against her, licking and sucking on her labia. But once a bitter taste fills her mouth, she backs away. She looks down to see a pool of yellow mucous oozing down Rachel's inner thighs.

"Keep going," Rachel whines, pushing herself into her mouth.

Addy can't deny her. She opens her mouth wider and saturates her tongue with the thick yellow gravy, trying to ignore the cancerous fishy flavor.

"Eat me," Rachel cries, moaning in ecstasy.

As Addy moves her tongue quicker, she tightens her grip on the back of Rachel's thighs. She can feel the creatures writhing beneath Rachel's skin, pushing on her fingers and against the palms of her hands as though they are desperate to get out.

The yellow fluid gushes out in thicker streams the closer Rachel comes to climaxing. When one of the parasites squeezes out of her against Addy's chin, the girl pulls back. She looks down at the fetus-like creature in shock. She's never actually seen one before. Its mouth gapes open, staring up at her with its beady black eyes. The fat little grub is covered in grease and foam, reaching out with its disturbingly human arm-like appendages.

Rachel snatches the fetus worm up in her fingers and pulls it to her left breast, rubbing its grease against her nipple.

"Keep eating me. I'm almost there."

Before Addy can react, Rachel shoves her face into her crotch with all her strength and orgasms against her.

"Eat me!" she screams.

A flood of fishy ooze fills Addy's mouth, along with two or three of the fetus worms.

"Eat them!" Rachel cries.

Addy coughs and gags as the parasites squirm down her throat. Rachel continues to orgasm, sending more of them inside of her.

"Yes!" Rachel yells, crushing the grub against her breast and smearing its insides across her body.

Addy tries to pull away, but there's nothing she can do. Five more worm their way into her mouth and she just swallows them, no longer able to resist. When Rachel is finished, she collapses on top of Addy and holds her tightly, breathing deeply against her.

"Holy shit, that was so hot," Rachel says.

Addy just nods and spits the fishy snot from her mouth. She's terrified of the parasites that have entered her body, but isn't sure what to do about them. She hopes they aren't dangerous.

Rachel rubs Addy's stomach and says, "You'll be having my babies soon." Then she giggles.

Addy is disturbed by her words at first, but after thinking about it for a moment she begins to smile. The idea makes her happy. Having Rachel's parasites might bring them closer. She doesn't mind dealing with the discomfort of being infected by the strange creatures as long as they'll make Rachel love her more. So far, Rachel has been fine despite how many are living inside of her. She's lost a lot of weight despite eating twice as much as she used to. She looks better than ever. Perhaps the parasites are more of a blessing than a curse.

They hold each other gently, bathing in the moonlight, feeling the squirming creatures beneath Rachel's skin. The ocean breeze caresses them. The boat rocks them gently back and forth.

After a few minutes of lingering in the afterglow, Rachel realizes that the boat isn't moving anymore. The engine isn't running. It's just drifting gently, pulled along by the waves.

Rachel looks around, wondering what's going on. Then she meets eyes with Blaise. The asshole is standing in the shadows on the other side of the dock, drinking a freshly opened bottle of scotch. She has no idea how long he's been there. Based on the angry look in his eyes, she's sure that he was watching them the entire time.

⚓

Before Rachel can say anything, Blaise flips out. He shouts and screams incoherent words at her and throws his bottle of liquor in her direction. It shatters at her feet and the glass sprays up at them. Conner wakes up to the noise.

"Blaise, calm down…" Rachel calls out to him, putting her

breasts back into her bikini top.

But he's not listening. He storms below deck and grabs both Rachel's and Addy's luggage and then throws it all overboard.

"What the fuck!" Rachel yells.

She runs to the side of the ship and looks over the side, seeing all of her stuff floating away.

"Fucking bitch!" Blaise says. "You think you can fuck with Daddy Cool?"

Rachel pushes him. "My phone and laptop were in there, asshole!"

Blaise stumbles back a little and then straightens himself. He gets in her face. "I bought you that phone and that laptop."

"I don't fucking care," Rachel yells.

Blaise points at Addy. "How can you do that to me? Do you think you can just fuck your friend on my boat without pissing me off?"

Rachel says, "Hey, you were throwing yourself a pity party and hiding from us all night. What's it matter to you? Besides, guys usually get turned on when they see their girlfriend making out with another woman."

"Bullshit!" Blaise yells. "Daddy Cool doesn't share his bitches with anyone, not even other girls."

Addy doesn't know how to respond to all of this. She stands back, not wanting to get involved. Conner, on the other hand, is taking off his watch and gold chain necklace, getting ready to throw down if he has to.

"You're such a fucking prick," Rachel says. "We never said our relationship is exclusive. If it was it would've cost you a lot more than you spent on me."

This pisses Blaise off even more. "You think you're worth more than that? You're not even slightly worth what I've paid to put you through school. I only did that because I cared about you. You're just a worthless trashy skank. I have no idea what I ever saw in you."

Rachel laughs in his face. "The feeling's mutual, you uptight douche. You think you're the shit because you have money and a yacht. You're just a self-centered old man with a weird penis who thinks he's god's gift to women even though everyone laughs about you behind your back."

Blaise's face turns red. He points in her face and says, "You take that back! I'm so not old and you said you loved my penis!"

"I've said a lot of things," Rachel says. "Do you really think I meant any of it?"

Blaise shoves Rachel. Then he grabs her by the arm and raises his fist, getting ready to punch her.

When Conner sees this, he charges at the guy and grabs him off of Rachel. He throws Blaise to the deck of his ship and gets between them.

"Do you think I'll let you touch my sister, asshole?" Conner yells. "I'll break both of your arms if you lay another finger on her."

Blaise is too trashed to fight the guy. He can barely get himself to his feet. "This is my boat, you little shit. You want to swim home?" As he gets up, Blaise tries to sucker punch the kid. But he's too old and drunk to get a proper swing in. Conner just steps aside and the guy falls back to the ground.

Rachel looks down at his pathetic sugar daddy and says, "It's over between us. We're done. Once you sober up, I want you to turn this boat around and take us home."

Blaise gets on his hands and knees and just screams, howling in frustration. Then he looks up at the college girl with fuming red eyes and says, "Nobody breaks up with Daddy Cool."

Rachel and Conner laugh at him.

Conner kicks him in the stomach and knocks him back down. "More like Daddy *Fool*." Then he high-fives his sister and spits on the deck. "What a fucking loser."

Blaise has never been more angry in his life. He gets to his feet, holding his stomach. Then he stumbles away. The college kids laugh and holler at him, yelling out insults about how old and pathetic and ugly he is. But Blaise doesn't let them get away with it. He rips open a case full of scuba gear and grabs a diving speargun. When he returns, he points the weapon at Conner and threatens him with it.

"Get off my ship, motherfucker!" Blaise yells.

Conner's eyes widen at the sight of the weapon. He holds up his hands and says in a panic, "Dude! Watch out with that thing. It's dangerous."

Blaise flexes his muscles, straightening his back to look as tough as he can in his drunken state. "Damn right, it's dangerous! I'm going to shoot you with it if you don't get the fuck off my boat."

"I can't get off the boat," Conner says. "We're in the middle of the fucking ocean."

"Take the dinghy," Blaise says. "I'll tell the Coast Guard to pick you up."

Conner says. "That's illegal man. It's murder. You can't kick someone off in the middle of the sea."

"I can if it's self defense. You attacked me."

Conner begs for mercy. "I'm sorry, man. I was just standing up for my sister."

Rachel tries to get involved. She goes to her sugar daddy and says, "Calm down. Just take us back to the dock and we'll leave."

Blaise turns to Rachel and points the speargun at her. "You're going with him, bitch. All three of you are leaving."

Rachel shakes her head. "Don't be crazy. We'll never make it."

Blaise chuckles. "Not my problem, skank. You should have treated Daddy Cool with some respect."

With the speargun pointed at Rachel, Conner takes the opportunity to strike. He lunges at Blaise and grabs the weapon, pushing it away from his sister. Blaise doesn't let go of the trigger, grabbing the barrel with his free hand and trying to pull it back.

"Let go, motherfucker!" Conner yells.

The two fight over the weapon, thrashing it in the air. Rachel and Addy step away, moving behind cover.

"You're fucking dead, you little shit!" Blaise yells.

Blaise kicks the college guy in the testicles, loosening his grip on the weapon. But before he can aim it back at him, his finger pulls the trigger. The spear flies across the deck and lands with a thud in a thick, meaty target.

All of them look over to Lily who has recently come from below deck to see what the commotion was all about. None of them noticed her there until it was too late. The spear has impaled her chest. She just looks in her father's eyes with shock and disgust as she falls to the ground.

⚓

"Holy shit!" Rachel cries.

The fight between Blaise and the college kids ends in an instant, all four of them more concerned for the girl than their petty squabble. They rush to Lily's side, filled with panic and worry.

Blaise goes to his daughter, yelling, "Oh my god! Oh my god! Oh my god!"

Lily coughs up blood, holding the spear in her chest.

Blaise puts his hands under her back and pulls her close to him, tears flowing from his eyes. "I'm so sorry, baby girl. Daddy Cool didn't mean it. It was just an accident. Daddy Cool would never hurt you."

Blood trickles down Lily's chin as she says, "Stop calling yourself Daddy Cool, asshole."

Blaise looks at Addy and says, "Get the first aid kit. It's over there under the seat. He points out the first aid box to the college girl and she goes straight for it.

"You're going to be okay," Blaise tells his daughter. "Don't worry. You'll be fine."

Rachel doesn't know what to do. She stands there shocked at

what has just occurred. Her brother goes to the girl and applies pressure to the wound, trying to stop the bleeding.

Not knowing what else to do, Rachel says, "I'll radio for help."

Then she races off toward the bridge, not even sure she'll know how to operate the radio equipment. But she has to get out of there. She can't be there if the kid dies in her father's arms. Even though she didn't lay a hand on the speargun, she can't help but think it's her fault somehow. She knows that the girl needs to get to a hospital quickly if she's going to survive. But out in the ocean, she doesn't know if it's possible. She has to get a hold of the Coast Guard. They have to know what to do in situations like this. If she doesn't do something soon that young girl is going to die.

⚓

Rachel goes to the bridge of the ship, hoping she'll be able to figure out how to call for help. But when she enters the cockpit, she can't believe her eyes. The controls are smashed. It's like somebody took an axe to it and destroyed everything.

Her jaw drops open. "What the fuck?"

The thought of some kind of axe murderer hiding on board comes to her mind, but she quickly shakes off that theory. After noticing the empty bottle of scotch and thinking it over for a moment, the reason the controls are smashed becomes clear. Blaise was hiding in here for hours after she rejected his marriage proposal. It's just like him to throw a tantrum and smash up his own ship's controls just because he didn't get his way. He probably wanted to get them stuck in the middle of the ocean so that she wouldn't be able to go back home until she agreed to become his wife.

"Fucking asshole…" Rachel says. "I'm going to kill that son of a bitch."

If he knew what was going to happen to his daughter he never would have done such a thing. He was acting emotionally and irrationally like he always does. Since there's no way to call for help, there's very little chance that the child is going to survive.

When Rachel goes back to the others, he sees Lily lying unconscious in her father's arms. At first, she thinks the girl is dead but then notices her still breathing. Her brother and girlfriend are standing back, staring at the child, not sure what to do. They don't want to pull the spear out of her chest. They're sure it will kill her if they do.

"What the fuck, Blaise?" Rachel yells, charging toward him. "You smashed the controls."

Blaise looks at her with a confused face, not sure what she's talking about. But after a moment of thought, the memories of his drunken rage fill his head. He puts his face in his hand and yells, "Fuck!"

"Were you trying to strand us out here as punishment for me rejecting you?" she asks him.

He shakes his head. "I was pissed off. Sorry."

She points at Lily. "How are we going to get your daughter help?"

Blaise takes a deep breath and thinks about it for a minute.

"It's fine," he says. "We still have the satellite phone. Where is it?"

"What?" Rachel asks. "You mean the one you gave me?"

Blaise gets annoyed with her. "Yes. The fucking expensive satellite phone you wanted that I bought you. Give it to me and I'll call for help."

Rachel groans at him. "The one that was in my luggage that you threw overboard?"

Blaise's face goes blank when he realizes what he's done. He doesn't respond to her.

"Was that the only satellite phone on board?" Rachel asks. "Why didn't you buy one for yourself?"

"Because I already bought one for you!" he yells.

"Fuck!" Rachel says, turning away from him.

She tries to calm down, not wanting to argue.

"Jesus Christ…" she says, turning back to him. "What are we going to do? If we can't get help she's going to die."

Blaise won't believe there's no hope. He shakes his head.

"It'll be fine," he says. "We got the bleeding to stop. She's not going to die."

"She needs medical attention," Rachel says.

"She needs you to shut the fuck up!" Blaise yells.

Rachel doesn't argue any further. She turns away from him. There's nothing they can do. The girl is going to die and it's all that asshole's fault.

⚓

Rachel, Addy and Conner stay far away from Blaise and Lily, sitting on the opposite side of the ship. They don't want to be anywhere near the girl when she dies. It's going to happen soon. All of them know it. But they don't think they have it in them to see a little girl die.

"This is so fucked up," Addy says, staring at her feet.

Conner takes a drag from his joint and exhales. Then he says, "Yeah. And I'm going to make sure that guy goes to jail for it when we get home. Fuck him."

"Are you sure we're going to make it home?" Rachel asks. "We've been set adrift. If we can't get help for the girl we also can't get help for ourselves."

Conner shrugs. "We're only half a day from the coast. I'm sure someone will pick us up."

"We've also got plenty of food," Addy mentions. "We can stretch it out for a long time."

Rachel touches her stomach, feeling the parasites crawling under her skin. Normally, they could stretch the amount of food they have for weeks. But Rachel isn't able to starve herself since she has been infected by the fetus worms. She's had to eat three times as much as she usually does in order to prevent the parasites from damaging her body. The creatures are ravenous. Eating a normal amount of food would leave her malnourished. If she ate no food at all, the worms would devour her body from the inside out. She doesn't have weeks. She has days at best.

"We've got to have some kind of emergency beacon," Rachel says. "Even if the controls are smashed, there's got to be a way to signal for help."

"What about the dinghy?" Conner asks. "If the ship is sinking and you have to evacuate on the dinghy, there's got to be something to signal for help. We can't possibly be screwed."

Rachel nods. "I'm sure Blaise will know what to do. Let's wait until he's in his right mind and then we'll get him to help us."

Conner shakes his head. "There's no way we can rely on that asshole. We should do it ourselves."

"He'll know better than us," Rachel says. "He's an asshole, but he'll want to get rescued more than any of us. He thinks he's god's gift to the world. There's no way he'll just let himself die."

"You think he's going to be so accommodating once his daughter dies?" Conner asks. "It's his food and water. It's his ship. He's not going to give a shit about helping us."

"Just be respectful," Rachel says. "He's not that bad of a guy when you get to know him. As long as we act like we're on his side he'll help us." She takes the joint from Conner and takes a drag. "Besides, if he doesn't want to go to jail for murdering his daughter, he'll want us as witnesses. We can reason with him."

Conner shakes his head. "I doubt that."

"Trust me," Rachel says. "We'll make it out of this alive as long as we play nice."

The other two look away, peering into the starlit sky. They don't feel as confident as Rachel is. They think they are royally screwed, whether they get Blaise's help or not.

⚓

The sun is rising over the horizon and none of them have moved from their spots. None of them have been able to sleep. It's just been too stressful of a night. Blaise is still holding his daughter on the other side of the ship, rocking her back and forth, talking to her about random things that no one else can hear.

Conner gets up from his seat and stretches. He goes to the railing of the ship and looks across the water.

Rachel makes eye contact with her girlfriend. The two of them stare at each other for a moment, and then take each other's hand. They lean against one another. Addy rests her head on Rachel's shoulder.

"We're going to get through this," Rachel says.

Addy lets out a sigh but doesn't respond. She's too worried to lie to herself about the danger they're in. None of them have ever been out on the ocean before. None of them have any idea what they can do or how much their lives are at stake. They made a bad decision going out on a boat with a complete asshole. They are sure that it will take a whole lot of luck to get them home safe.

"Hey, what the fuck is that?" Conner asks.

Rachel lifts her head and looks at her brother. He's staring at something off on the horizon. The two women get up and go to him. They see something out there. Something large.

"Doesn't that look like a ship to you?" Conner asks, squinting his eyes at the object.

Rachel can't be sure. She just watches the thing in the distance until it continues on its path toward them.

"I think it is!" Addy cries, a smile curling on her face.

Rachel shakes her head. "I don't know. It could be anything."

"Bullshit," Conner says. "That's definitely a boat."

Rachel lets out a sigh. "I'm going to get Blaise."

The others look at her with concern, but they don't volunteer to go with her.

Conner looks back at the object in the distance. "It's coming right for us. They're going to see us for sure."

"Do you think it's the Coast Guard?" Addy asks.

Conner isn't sure. "It looks too big to be a Coast Guard ship."

"I'll be back," Rachel says, heading in the direction of Blaise and his daughter.

⚓

Blaise is still holding his daughter in his arms. His face is red and puffy. He doesn't have any tears left to cry. Rachel is half-expecting to see Lily dead when she arrives, but the girl is still breathing. Her eyes are flickering and her lips are moving, as though she's in the middle of a very intense dream.

Blaise looks up at Rachel. There's very little life in his eyes, completely destroyed by what has happened to him.

"There's something coming toward us," Rachel tells him. "It looks like a boat. We might be able to get help."

When she says this, Blaise's eyes light up. "Are you serious?"

Rachel nods.

"Oh my god," he says. "We need to get the flares."

He gently picks his daughter off his lap and sets her head on the deck of the ship. Then he kisses her on the forehead and says, "We're going to get you help, baby girl. Just you wait."

⚓

When Rachel and Blaise return to the others, they clearly see the ship heading in their direction. Only a sliver of the sun has risen from the horizon, so there's not enough light to fully see the vessel. But it's definitely a boat. It definitely will be able to help them out.

"It looks like a cruise ship," Conner says to Rachel when she comes up behind him.

"That's perfect," Blaise says. "They'll have a doctor on board."

When the boat comes in close enough, Blaise shoots a flare into the air. It illuminates the morning sky and gives them a better view of the vessel heading toward them. The four of them watch as the flare falls in the distance.

"Do you think they saw it?" Addy asks.

"They had to have," Conner says. "Do you know how many people are on a cruise ship? They probably saw us long before we saw them."

Blaise isn't going to risk it. This ship is his only chance to save his daughter. He shoots another flare, right in the direction of the ship.

"Don't waste them," Rachel says.

But Blaise doesn't care. He shoots them one after another. Just as he sends the last one up, he says, "If they don't pick us up Lily's going to die. There's no way I'm going to risk them missing us."

"How do we know if they see us?" Addy asks. "Is there some kind of signal to let us know?"

"They see us," Blaise says. "They have to."

⚓

For the next ten minutes, they just watch the ship approach, waiting in desperation for rescue to arrive. But the ship isn't slowing down. There's no way to tell if it has any intention of giving them a lift.

When it comes closer, within a hundred feet, Blaise's eyes sink. There seems to be something off about the cruise ship. There are no lights coming from any of the windows or the bridge. The exterior is coated in rust and cracks. Many of the windows have been shattered. It doesn't appear to have any sign of life whatsoever.

"What the hell is that thing?" Rachel asks.

Everyone is thinking the same thing. It's definitely not normal. The cruise ship's engine isn't running. They are just as adrift as the yacht.

"Is it a ghost ship?" Conner asks. "It looks like a wreck."

Blaise shakes his head. "Ghost ships don't exist. Not anymore. With modern technology, there's no way a boat that big could be lost at sea. It has to be a normal cruise ship that's just seen better days."

"Who the hell would buy a ticket on a boat in that shape?" Rachel asks.

Blaise shrugs. "Maybe somebody bought an old cruise ship and is testing it out to see if it's still seaworthy."

"Yeah, somebody's got to be on board," Conner says.

They all stand there waiting, but the cruise ship doesn't show any sign of life. It heads straight for them, on a collision course.

"Oh shit, it's going to hit us!" Rachel yells.

"Brace yourselves," Blaise says.

The cruise ship rams *The Crotch Moistener* and knocks them all off their feet. Blaise's ship is crumpled against the hull of the massive ocean liner, bending it in the middle.

When Blaise gets to his feet, he looks over at his daughter to make sure she's okay. But she's not been disturbed by the impact. He goes to the side of his boat and looks down.

"We're taking on water," he says. "We have to get off or we're going to sink."

The cruise ship continues on its way, pushing the yacht out of its way. Blaise's boat scrapes against the side of the ocean liner, making a squealing noise so loud that they can barely hear each other.

"How?" Rachel cries. "What do we do?"

"Get the anchor," Blaise says. "We need to get on board the ship."

Rachel looks around, confused about where to get the anchor. But Blaise goes for it in her stead.

"We have to connect ourselves to the boat before it gets away," Blaise says.

He gets the anchor and holds it up over his shoulder. He tries throwing it at the cruise ship, trying to latch it onto something. But he's not strong enough to get it more than three feet in the air.

"Let me do it," Conner tells him.

Blaise lets the college kid give it a try.

"It's almost thirty pounds," Blaise says. "I don't know if it will work."

But Conner is far more athletic than the middle-aged man. He can throw a shot put twenty meters. The anchor is twice the weight of a shot put, but if he can throw it as high as ten meters he should be able to make it work.

"Aim for the windows," Blaise yells, pointing at the shattered openings closest to the water.

Conner throws the anchor up high enough to reach the closest window, but it doesn't connect. He tries again, but it's a couple meters too short. By the third attempt, his strength is failing him. He's already strained himself with the first two throws, pulling a muscle in his arm. The third attempt barely makes it over the railing of the yacht.

"I don't think it's possible," Conner says, breathing heavily.

"You have to try!" Rachel yells. "It's our only chance."

"Aim for the gangway!" Blaise yells, pointing at a staircase running along the outer side of the ship.

Before the ship passes, Conner gives it one last effort. He throws the anchor with every ounce of strength in his body at the gangway as it passes them. The anchor connects, hooking on one of the steps.

The rest of them cheer. Rachel and Addy squeeze Conner

on the shoulders as he grips the chain in his hands. He pumps his fist, relieved he was able to actually make it happen. With the ships linked together, there's no way they'll be able to drift apart. But *The Crotch Moistener* is still sinking. They have to get off soon.

⚓

"Hello?" Rachel yells up to the cruise ship. "Is anyone there?"

But there's no response.

Their yacht rocks and sways in the sea, slamming into the side of the cruise ship, tugging on the gangway that connects them by a chain.

"We're not going to stay attached forever," Blaise says. "We should get on board."

"Sounds like a plan to me, bro," Conner says.

Blaise turns to Rachel and tells her and Addy to get as many supplies as possible from the kitchen and below deck. Just in case the ship is abandoned, they're going to need food and water. Then he tells Conner to get on board and ask for help while he gets his daughter. They all agree to the plan and take action.

When they're ready to board the rusty old cruise ship, Rachel looks up at the massive vessel. She doesn't think the ship looks all that safe but she knows it's their only choice. She only hopes that Blaise is right, that it's not a ghost ship. She hopes they can get help for the girl. She hopes that they will find people who will get them back to land. She hopes that the worst of this terrible experience is already behind them.

CHAPTER THREE
CONNER

⚓

Conner is the first to board the cruise ship. He hops over the railing onto the gangway while the others are busy getting their things together. Then he climbs the stairs up to the main level of the vessel.

There's nobody waiting for him once he arrives. The atrium of the ship is vacant, filled with old trash and discarded luggage that looks like it's been sitting there for years.

"Hello?" Conner calls out. "Is anyone there? We need help."

But the only sound that responds is that of an old ship creaking and whistling in the ocean breeze. He looks down at *The Crotch Moistener*, but there's nobody in sight. All of them must be below deck gathering their supplies.

Conner decides to explore further. He finds a staircase heading up to the main deck. The second he sees it, he's sure the ship has to be abandoned. The chairs are broken to pieces. The pool is empty but for a large puddle of black sludge. The floor of the deck is coated in garbage and rust-colored grime. There's no way this boat has been used for a luxury cruise in a very long time. But he doesn't want to give up. He hopes that somebody is on board, sailing the ship.

"Hello?" he calls out again. "This is an emergency."

It seems to be no use. Nobody comes out of hiding. The place has to be abandoned.

⚓

Conner goes back downstairs and waits for the others to come aboard.

They don't seem too happy when he says, "Nobody's here. It's completely empty."

Rachel and Addy are concerned by his words, but Blaise doesn't believe him.

"There's got to be somebody," Blaise says, carrying his daughter in his arms, the spear still sticking out of her chest. "Have you checked the bridge?"

"I don't know where it is," Conner says.

Blaise sighs and says, "I'll come with you to find it." Then looks at Rachel and says, "Can you take her to the medbay?" He holds Lily out to his young girlfriend and she reluctantly takes the child, careful not to hurt her with the spear in her chest.

"How do I get to the medbay?" Rachel asks.

"Follow the signs," he tells her, pointing at the walls that give directions to those seeking medical attention.

Rachel nods and goes in the direction of the signs. Addy follows close behind her, brushing Lily's hair out of her eyes.

⚓

"You're with me," Blaise tells Conner.

Conner nods. Even though they were ready to kill each other the night before, they have no problem working together now that lives are at stake. Conner follows the douche bag across the abandoned deck toward the front of the ship. But the deeper into the ship they go, the more he realizes there's definitely something wrong with this boat. As they go down a hallway, heading toward the bridge, something that looks like blood has been splashed across the walls. It's long dried and more of a brownish color, but it definitely looks like blood. Many of the doors have been broken off their hinges to reveal toppled furniture and ripped up bedding. Some of the doors look like they were chopped down by axes.

"What happened here?" Conner asks.

But Blaise doesn't respond. He doesn't care about the state of the ship. He only cares about what happens to his daughter. He knows he's been a shitty father to her, too absorbed in his own self-interests to give her the upbringing she needed. But if he can get her through this he plans to make everything better. He plans to be the best father he can be for the girl. He doesn't care that her mother hates him. He doesn't care that everyone in his life thinks he's the biggest piece of shit they've ever known. He can change. He can prove everyone wrong. As long as his daughter pulls through, he knows that he can turn it all around.

"This isn't a modern cruise ship, is it?" Conner asks. "Everything looks so old. Like it's from the '90s."

"It seems older than that," Blaise says. "The 1960s or 1970s. It hasn't operated as a cruise ship for a very long time."

"But you still think other people are on board?" Conner asks.

Blaise nods. "Somebody has to have made this thing seaworthy. It's too old to have been adrift so long. We're less than a day from the coast. I'm sure somebody is at the wheel."

Conner doesn't know if he believes the middle-aged man, but he follows after him anyway. They'll know soon enough once they reach the bridge.

⚓

There isn't anyone at the helm when Blaise and Conner finally reach the bridge. The place is empty. A breeze blows in from a broken window. Not a soul in sight.

"It doesn't look like anyone's been in here for a long time," Conner says.

Blaise is more shocked by this discovery than the college kid. He says, "It's impossible. How could a cruise ship this size be abandoned?"

"Who the fuck knows?" Conner says, knocking on a rusted control panel. "But there's obviously been no one driving this thing for a very long time."

Blaise shakes his head, refusing to believe it.

"Maybe somebody just stepped away from the controls," Blaise says. "There could be a small crew who drank too much and are sleeping it off below deck. Just because the ship is old and in disrepair doesn't mean that nobody else is here. It could have been rotting in a dock somewhere for decades up until a few days ago. I'm sure somebody else is on board."

Conner shrugs. "If you say so."

He doesn't want to disillusion the guy. Blaise is in a desperate situation. Conner knows that it's going to take a lot before the old guy gives up hope.

Instead of trying to convince him the ship is deserted, Conner looks for some kind of clues to what might have happened here. He finds a travel brochure in a drawer that must have been given to passengers a long time ago. As he thumbs through it, Blaise focuses on figuring out how the ship works. Everything is so old that he doesn't know exactly what anything does. He wonders if there's a way he can call for help.

"*The Pacific Princess…*" Conner says as he reads the travel brochure. "That sounds familiar, doesn't it?"

Blaise lets out a laugh. "Yeah, that would be hilarious, wouldn't it?"

Conner is confused. "Have you heard of it before?"

"*The Pacific Princess?*" Blaise asks. "Of course I have."

Conner holds up the brochure. "That's the name of this ship."

Blaise doesn't believe him. He takes the brochure out of his hand and looks it over. Then he examines the ship and finds other evidence that the boat is indeed *The Pacific Princess*.

"It's impossible…" Blaise says.

"What's impossible?" Conner asks.

Blaise looks at him. "*The Pacific Princess* is the ship that was the basis of the show *The Love Boat* show from the 1970s. All the exterior shots were filmed on this very ship."

"You're saying this ship is the fucking *Love Boat*?"

Blaise shakes his head. "*The Love Boat* was fictional. But there was a ship that it was filmed on, that inspired the story. *The Pacific Princess* was that ship."

Conner shrugs. "I don't know, dude. I never watched it. My parents were kids when that show was on."

Blaise is getting excited. "But what's more crazy is that there's a rumor that the original *Pacific Princess*, the one that they filmed the first season on, was lost at sea. They say that the studio and the cruise line covered it up. Supposedly, they just took an identical ship and renamed it *The Pacific Princess* so that it wouldn't hurt publicity for the show. I mean, Princess Cruises became a huge company after the success of the television series. It makes sense that they would have buried what happened here." Blaise smiles. "I can't believe that it's true."

Everything Blaise said went over Conner's head. "Are you saying we're standing on the set of a '70s sitcom?"

Blaise shakes his head. "It's just the ship they filmed the first season on. If this ship really is abandoned, if it actually is lost at sea, we've just stumbled on one of the biggest mysteries of the past fifty years."

Conner doesn't understand. "So how does that help us?"

Blaise shrugs. "It means we're going to be rich."

"Aren't you already rich?" Conner asks.

Blaise laughs. "Not as rich as we're about to become."

And then they both freak out in excitement. They high-five each other, thrilled that they've made the discovery of the century. But once they think about it for a moment, realizing that finding a legendary ship that was lost at sea isn't actually going to save them, their smiles turn to frowns. They still have to get help. They still need to save Lily's life. Just because they are on the original *Pacific Princess* doesn't mean their problems have gone away.

⚓

After fidgeting with the controls for ten minutes, Blaise realizes there's nothing he can do. Everything is dirty and rusted and fifty years out of date. He won't be able to get help on his own. They decide to go back to the others and see how Lily is doing. Perhaps there's a way that they can help the girl on their own. If they have the right medical equipment, they might be able to remove the spear and stop the bleeding themselves.

When they get to the medbay, Blaise and Conner are shocked to see that Lily is conscious and sitting upright on a bed. She's chatting with Rachel and Addy, smiling and joking around with them. If it wasn't for the spear sticking out of her chest, she would have appeared to be the picture of health.

"Oh my god, baby girl!" Blaise cries when he sees her. "You're awake!"

Lily groans at her father. "No thanks to you."

He rushes to her and forces her into a hug, nearly pushing the spear deeper into her chest.

"Daddy Cool was so worried," he says, hugging her as tight as he can.

Lily just sighs in irritation as she lets her father hug him.

"She's gotten a lot better since she came on board," Rachel says. "I think she'll pull through."

"We still need a doctor to get the spear out of her," Addy says. "Have you found anyone who can help us?"

Blaise shakes his head. "The ship is abandoned. It doesn't seem like anyone is on board."

Addy looks at the girl. "What are we going to do?"

Blaise says, "We have to do it ourselves. We need to remove the spear."

Conner shakes his head. "That's too dangerous, man. It could be all that's keeping her alive."

"We've got to try," Blaise says. "This place has everything we need, doesn't it?"

They look around the medbay. It's just a small room, just enough to work on a single patient at a time. But the cabinets are fully stocked. Even though everything is fifty years old, there's plenty of supplies to help the girl.

"But we need a doctor," Addy says. "We can't do this on our own."

Rachel shakes her head. "We have a doctor."

She looks at her brother.

Conner shakes his head.

"You can do it," Rachel says. "I'm sure you can."

Conner holds up his hands. "Fuck no. No way."

She explains to the others. "Conner's in pre-med. He's studying to be a doctor."

"I'm not a doctor," he says. "Mom and Dad want me to be, but I'm not going to medical school. Fuck that. I'm only taking pre-med to shut them up."

"But you're better equipped than anyone else to deal with this," Rachel says.

Conner holds up his hands and takes a step back. "I'm a shitty student, though. I haven't taken my classes seriously. I don't know any better than any of you. I can't do it."

None of them believe him. They all look at him like he's their only hope. If Conner could help the girl he would have done it back on the yacht.

Blaise looks at the college guy, pleading him with his eyes. "You can do it, can't you? You can save my daughter?"

Conner shakes his head. "I told you, I can't. You're better off doing it yourself."

Blaise won't let it go. "You've got to do it. Please. I'm begging you."

Conner breaks eye contact. He can't believe he's been put in this position. There's no good outcome to it. If he runs away and the girl dies, they will all blame him for her death. If he operates on her and she dies, they will all blame him for her death. It's a lose-lose for Conner.

"Just give it a shot," Rachel tells him. "We don't have a choice."

Lily looks at Rachel and says, "Are you sure? He seems like kind of a fuckup."

Conner points at her. "That's right. I'm a total fuckup!"

But nobody else will let him out of it. He has no choice but to take on the entire responsibility of saving the girl's life, even though he has no idea how he'll be able to do it.

⚓

Conner isn't concerned about his ability to help the girl because he's a bad pre-med student. He's mostly concerned because he doesn't remember the majority of the classes he's taken.

No one is aware of it, but Conner suffers from multiple personality disorder. He actually has one hundred and fifty different personalities all living in the same body. But why nobody has noticed this fact is because every single personality of his are exactly the same as the last. They are all the same intolerable college bro who likes to party and hang out without their shirts on. They all drink cheap beer and smoke joints. They all hit on girls in an exceptionally creepy way. Not a single one of them is a worthwhile human being.

This is why he's such a terrible pre-med student. He's a different personality with every class he's taken, and not a single personality has been bothered to share the information they've learned with any of the others. Even if his classes had taught him all he needs to know to fix the girl, he doesn't remember any of it.

But there's no way out of it. Conner has to be the one to operate. He has to wing it, hoping that he can do the job based on movies and television shows he's seen in the past. He goes to the supply closet and is glad to see it's fully stocked. He decides that he needs rubbing alcohol, bandages, some rubber gloves and something to cut through the spear. There's a saw-like device that looks like it was designed to amputate an infected limb, but it's the only thing Conner can find that might cut through the spear.

"Hold her down," Conner says, once he washes his hands with rubbing alcohol and slips on the rubber gloves.

Rachel and Blaise grip Lily by the arms, but they don't restrain her too much, as though they don't want to hurt her.

Conner takes a deep breath and then goes to the girl. He pours rubbing alcohol on the saw and then brings it to the spear.

"Here goes nothing," he says, hoping all the movies he's seen on operating people in an emergency situation haven't steered him wrong.

But before he brings his saw to the girl, his personalities change to another version of Conner. This new version has no idea what the hell is going on. He notices the saw in his hand and the spear in the girl and goes into a panic.

"Holy shit…" Conner says, looking at his sister. "I think I need a joint."

"Fuck that," Blaise yells. "You have to do this sober."

Conner chuckles. "Too late, bro."

His sister looks him in the eyes and tells him, "You can do this. I believe in you."

Conner shrugs. The one thing that he's learned from living so many years with multiple personalities is that no matter what situation he's in, all he has to do is wing it. He just pretends that he knows what's going on and everything always tends to work out.

He brings the saw to the spear and cuts into it. The girl screams at the pain and the others hold her in place.

"Don't you have some kind of painkiller?" Lily asks.

Conner just shrugs and continues sawing. The girl shrieks at the top of her lungs.

"Be more gentle," Blaise tells the college kid.

"Don't worry, bro," Conner tells him. "I know what I'm doing."

But no matter how much he tries, he can't saw through the spear. In frustration, he drops the saw and grabs hold of the spear, then bends it in half. He breaks it off as the girl cries out in pain. Then he pulls it out of her back.

As blood gushes out of the wound, Conner pours rubbing alcohol over the girl's chest. Lily screams even louder. He quickly sews her up like he's stitching a hole in his boxer shorts and then does the same on her backside. He's not sure if that will actually stop the bleeding, but it's the most he can do.

Once he's finished, he cleans the blood off of her body and wraps her up in bandages. Then he steps back and nods his head in satisfaction.

"Can I light up a joint now?" Conner asks.

The others ignore him, too busy going to Lily to see if she's okay. The girl is ready to pass out from the pain, but otherwise she looks okay.

"You did it," Rachel says. "You saved her."

Conner just lights up his joint and shrugs. Then he takes a puff.

Blaise looks over at him and says, "Thanks, man. I owe you one."

And Conner gives him a thumbs up, even though he has no idea who the guy is.

⚓

When Conner changes back to his previous personality, he's shocked to see the operation is already over. He was just getting started and everything went blank. But seeing how everything seemed to work out, he's more than happy not to have experienced any of it. He's happy that one of his other personalities took over for him. Now he can just smoke his joint and relax.

"That was pretty amazing," Addy tells him. "I can't believe you were able to do that."

Conner just plays it off cool. "Well, I'm pre-med, you know. This was nothing."

But even though he's taking all the credit, Conner can't help but think he was not the one responsible for Lily's recovery. No matter which of his personalities helped the girl, Conner believes it was all Lily's doing. The kid is just tough. She's a survivor. She took a spear to the chest and wouldn't die. Just before the operation, she was acting like nothing happened. Conner's never seen anyone so tough, especially not some little girl. He didn't do anything. It's the kid's strength that saved her.

"What do we do now?" Rachel asks.

"We still need to get help," Blaise says.

They all agree.

Conner adds, "There's antibiotics in the cabinet. Your daughter will need them if it takes more than a day for us to get rescued."

Blaise nods his head at Conner, treating him like an expert. Conner just takes another drag of his joint, completely talking out of his ass. He's sure that the girl really does need antibiotics, but he has no idea what to do with them. If they've been on the ship for fifty years they're surely expired. But he isn't going to stop acting like he knows what he's talking about after receiving so much praise and appreciation.

"We should explore the ship more," Blaise says. "I doubt anyone else is on board but there's still a slight possibility. We have to be sure."

The others all agree with him. It's a large boat. They really don't know anything about the place yet, even if it seems to be completely deserted.

Blaise turns to Addy. "Can you stay here and watch my daughter while the rest of us look around?"

Addy nods her head. "Sure."

Lily objects. "I can go with you."

She tries to get on her feet, but her father pushes her back up on the operating table.

"No, stay here," Blaise says.

"I feel fine," Lily says. "Let me come too."

Blaise shakes his head. "You've got to rest. Let Daddy Cool handle this."

"I don't want to just wait around here. I want to search the ship with all of you."

Blaise ignores her and grows a stupid smile on his face. He says, "Daddy who?"

Lily groans. "Jesus Christ, I hate you."

"Daddy who?" Blaise asks again.

Lily just lets out a sigh and says, "Fine. Daddy Cool. Are you happy?"

Blaise winks at her. "Damn right."

Then Conner, Blaise, and Rachel leave the medbay, waving their goodbyes to Addy and Lily. They have a lot of ground to cover if they hope to search the entire vessel. If they're lucky they could have it all explored by midday.

"Let's go," Blaise says to the others.

And despite the fact that they hate the guy, both of them follow after him like a couple of lost little puppies.

⚓

Conner, Blaise and Rachel decide to stick together, none of them wanting to get lost on the enormous cruise ship. But as they explore, the more concerned they get with the vessel they've found themselves stranded on. There's so much damage to the ship that wasn't caused by rot or decay. Something very horrible happened here. So many doors have been smashed in. So many walls are covered in dried blood. It looks like a war broke out on the ship at some point, as though the boat was lost at sea and the passengers fought each other over supplies. But if that's the case, where are all the bodies? Why is the place so devoid of life?

"What do you think happened here?" Rachel asks, scanning the empty rooms as they go from deck to deck.

"It looks like there was a riot," Conner says.

Rachel shakes her head. "I don't like it one bit."

Blaise rolls his eyes at them. "It's no big deal. This kind of thing happens all the time on boats."

The two college kids look at him in bewilderment.

"What happens all the time?" Rachel asks. "People breaking down doors and covering the walls with blood?"

Blaise shrugs. "Shit goes down when you're out at sea. It doesn't take a lot for a riot to start. Clog a few toilets, run out of crab legs, tell people the pool is closed… you'd be surprised by what people will riot over. It's got to be hell to deal with passengers on a cruise ship."

The other two just laugh at him, not sure if he was serious or just joking. They decide to treat it like he meant the latter.

"What if it was something more serious than that?" Rachel asks. "What if a mass shooter was on board and took everyone out?"

Conner shakes his head. "There'd have to be a lot more people involved than a single shooter." He points at the ground.

"And there'd be a lot of shells lying around if somebody was actually using a gun."

Blaise doesn't humor them any further. He says, "There's no use speculating what happened. Whatever it was, it took place decades ago. It's no danger to us now."

"Are you sure about that?" Rachel asks.

"Hella sure," Blaise says. Then he smiles to her and grabs her around the shoulder, pulling her close to him.

Rachel's expression turns to disgust as he gropes her, but she doesn't stop him. It's almost as though he's ignoring the fact that they broke up the night before. Rachel isn't happy about it one bit. Because of what happened to his daughter, she's willing to keep the peace with him. But she still blames him for their situation. She has no intention of forgiving him.

Before she can wiggle out of his grip, Blaise lets her go and says, "Let's go down further. I want to take a look at the engine room."

Conner agrees. "Maybe this ship is still operational."

Blaise shrugs. "You never know. Ships this old were made to last."

The college students agree and follow Blaise toward a stairwell, heading deeper into the ship.

⚓

As they go to the lower decks, Rachel hears noises coming from the ship.

"Do you hear that?" Rachel asks the others.

The two men look at each other, but don't know what she's taking about. Rachel steps out of the stairwell, into the lowest deck that still has passenger quarters. The others follow her.

"What do you hear?" Conner asks.

"People," Rachel says. "It sounds like moaning."

Blaise shakes his head. "It's just your imagination. These

ships will do that."

Rachel shushes him. "I'm not imagining it. Just listen."

The two men go quiet and listen. They don't hear the moaning she's talking about, but they hear something.

"It sounds like rattling chains," Conner says.

But Blaise tells him to shut up and listens more carefully.

"I'm hearing a scraping sound," Blaise says.

"No, that's not what I'm talking about. There are people moaning out. It's like they're calling for help."

Blaise doesn't listen to her. "No, it's a scraping noise. It's probably my ship rubbing against the hull."

Rachel shakes her head. "It wasn't that. Keep listening."

But no matter how much the two men humor her, they don't hear anything.

"I think it's coming from the floor below," she says.

She goes back to the stairwell and goes down deeper. The two men follow her.

⚓

When they get to the bottom deck, everything changes. It doesn't even look like the same ship anymore. It's like a slaughterhouse. Chains and meat hooks hang from the ceiling, swaying back and forth with the rocking ship. Severed limbs and chunks of flesh are hanging from hooks. There are instruments of torture scattered about the place. Whips, racks, iron maidens, spikes and nooses. It must have been the engine room at one point but it's been converted into some kind of dark, dingy torture dungeon. They've never seen anything so horrific in all their lives.

As the three of them enter the area, they are hit by an intense odor like animal shit and rotting flesh. Rachel is so overwhelmed by the odor that she dry heaves into a corner and spits thick fluids onto a pile of old clothing. The two men just cover their noses with their hands and move forward.

"I guess we know what happened to all the passengers," Conner says, pointing at rows upon rows of animal cages.

Inside of the cages are naked bodies, hundreds of them, all piled up and rotting in the hot room.

"Fuck…" Blaise says. "This is messed up."

Rachel shakes her head. "I don't like this. We should go."

The two men don't share her sense of danger and explore further.

"How come they're so fresh?" Conner asks.

Blaise looks over at him with a confused expression.

"You said this ship was lost at sea since the early seventies," Conner explains. "If these are the original passengers then how come their bodies are in such good condition? They look like they died only days ago. A week at most."

Blaise doesn't know how to explain it. "Maybe they survived for a long time on this ship."

"Fifty years?" Conner asks. "These can't be the original passengers."

Blaise raises his eyebrows. "What do you think then?"

"I don't know, man," Conner says. "Maybe somebody found *The Pacific Princess* at sea decades ago and turned it into a black market slave ship. Maybe something happened in transit and the crew had to evacuate, leaving their human cargo to die."

Blaise thinks about it for a minute and says, "There weren't any lifeboats on the main deck. It's possible something like that happened."

Rachel doesn't agree with their story. "Why would there be all the torture devices if this ship was only transporting human cargo? Something sick was going on here."

Conner has an idea. "Have you seen the movie *Hostel*?" he asks them. They don't really know what he's talking about. "It's about rich people who pay money to torture and kill human slaves. What if this was the cruise ship version of that? Rich people pay for a luxury cruise and get to spend the whole trip torturing and mutilating these people locked down here. Some kind of sick bastard's version of a Disney cruise."

Rachel doesn't like any of the ideas her brother is coming up with. She says, "Whatever happened, we've got to get off this ship. It's not safe here. Let's just take the dinghy and go."

"We're fine for now," Blaise says. "The ship is abandoned. Whoever left isn't coming back."

"You don't know that," Rachel says. "If they find us on their ship we're fucked. Your daughter's been patched up. We have no reason to be here. We should go."

But Blaise doesn't listen to her. He continues walking down that passageway through the rows of cages, examining the bodies within. The prisoners have been torn apart. They have gashes and whip marks across their bodies. Many are missing limbs. Their guts are ripped out. A couple of them have been decapitated and their heads sewn to their own assholes, mouth-first. One woman was strangled by her own intestines cut from her abdomen. All the bodies are covered in blood and feces. Whatever happened here, it must have been absolute hell for every one of them.

"What's that?" Conner asks, pointing ahead of them.

The other two look. There's some kind of orange light emanating from the middle of the deck. They go toward it.

"Seriously, we should just go," Rachel says.

But the other two are too curious to let it go and she's too afraid to take off on her own.

When they get to the light, they find several crates filled with radiant orange crystals. They pulse and glow like neon lights. A type of mineral that none of them have seen or heard of before. Conner goes to the crystals and picks one of them up, examining it.

"It's warm," he says, lifting it up and down to feel its weight in his hand.

"Don't touch it," Rachel cries. "It could be radioactive."

Conner looks at Blaise. "What do you think it is?"

Blaise shrugs. "No idea. I've never seen anything like it."

"It could be valuable," Conner says, looking down at the twinkling rock.

"Or dangerous," Rachel says.

Conner puts it in his pocket. "Might as well try to sell it once we get home."

Rachel shakes her head. "You're such an idiot."

Conner shrugs. "If my hair and teeth start falling out I'll get rid of it."

Rachel just groans and looks behind them, realizing they've come so far that she can no longer see the exit.

"We should just go," she says.

"We will," Blaise says. "After we explore the rest of the deck."

Rachel can't believe they're being such idiots. After everything they've discovered, the only clear answer is to get the hell out of there.

⚓

Blaise examines the closest cage to them, filled with nearly twenty dead bodies. The glowing crystals illuminate this cell more than the others, so he's able to get a better view of the victims. They're all naked and horribly mutilated. They must have experienced unspeakable deaths at the hands of absolute monsters.

One female corpse is lying against the bars closest to Blaise. He kneels and examines her. There're so many cuts on her body that she looks fuzzy, all the scar tissue blending together into something like a sweater. When he sticks his finger through the bar and touches her, he's surprised to find that she's still warm.

"I think this one might still be alive," Blaise says.

He puts two fingers on the side of her neck and listens. The pulse is faint but it's there.

"She is!" he cries. "She's not dead."

Before he can pull his fingers away, the woman grabs him by the wrist and pulls his arm into the cage with her. She turns and looks at him with white empty eyes, as though somebody has poured boiling water in her eye sockets until it cooked the color out of them.

"Holy fuck!" Blaise screams, trying to get his hand back.

The woman shrieks, opening her mouth to expose black teeth and a stub of meat where her tongue used to be.

"She's alive!" Blaise cries.

But it's not just this woman. All of the bodies in all of the cages wake up and crawl toward the bars.

"They're all alive!" Rachel yells.

Blaise rips his hand out of the woman's grip and backs away.

Despite how scarred and mutilated they all are, every single prisoner is alive. They are missing limbs and are practically skin and bones, but none of them are dead. They were all just asleep, like they were hibernating.

The zombie-like people reach their hands through the bars, desperately grasping for those on the outside. Conner doesn't know if they are begging for help or if they mean them harm. But they don't want to stick around to see which is true.

⚓

"Let's get the fuck out of here!" Rachel yells.

The two men don't need any persuasion this time. They're both ready to run. However, they aren't sure which direction to escape in. They are in the middle of the ship with cages stretching in both directions, hundreds of arms reaching through the bars, blocking their way.

Instead of going back the way they came, where the arms are thicker and in greater number, they decide to move ahead.

They run through the skeletal arms of the prisoners, pushing past them with all their strength. Because the prisoners are so thin and weak, they are able to get through without getting grabbed.

"How the hell are they still alive?" Conner asks.

Rachel doesn't know either. She says, "Just keep going."

"They're like fucking zombies!" Conner yells.

"Just keep going," Rachel repeats.

But before they get to the other end of the ship, they see someone blocking their path. Blaise stops in his tracks, holding the others back.

When Rachel sees it, she says, "What the fuck is that?"

It's some kind of guard of the dungeon. A woman who's just as cut up and mutilated as those in the cells, but she's not a prisoner. She's a prison keeper.

She gets to her feet, stretching upward like some kind of possessed skeleton. The woman is tall, at least a foot taller than the men. She's knotty with muscle, not an ounce of fat on her body. She wears leather shorts and knee socks, black gloves on her hands. She's topless with long grubby breasts that dangle below her beltline. Barbell piercings through her nipples hold ten pound weights that cause her breasts to hang even farther down her body. She appears to be an old woman of at least seventy, but there's no wrinkles on her. She looks stronger and more fit than any of them.

"Holy shit…" Rachel says, when the woman turns toward them.

The woman faces them, wearing some kind of plate over her face that has been nailed to her skull. The plate features a picture of a man from the 1970s with a handsome smile and curly black hair.

"It's Gopher…" Blaise says.

The others ask what he's talking about.

Blaise points at the picture nailed to her head. "Gopher. A character from *The Love Boat*."

But he's not sure why the woman is wearing a picture of the head steward of *The Pacific Princess*. He wonders if it is some kind of cosplay, even though Gopher is male and this strange woman is obviously female. He also has no idea how the woman can see or breathe with a metal plate nailed to her face. She looks like some kind of monstrous creature with her curled, elongated spine and long bony arms. She lifts jagged metal blades that seem to have been made by hand out of metal pieces of the ship.

"That thing is fucked up," Conner says, not able to take his eyes off of her.

"Come on." Rachel grabs his brother by the shoulder. "We need to go."

But instead of going back the way they came, Blaise tells them to keep going forward. There's a stairwell between them and Gopher. It'll be quicker to escape if they go for that instead of trying the way they came. If any of them were to be grabbed by the people in the cages, they'd have no chance of escaping from the deranged Gopher woman.

⚓

Blaise, Rachel and Conner dash toward Gopher, screaming and yelling as though they're about to attack her. Gopher holds up her hands, raising her blades and listening to their footsteps as they come at her. But just before they make impact, Blaise turns and jumps into the stairwell. They all run up the steps, trying to escape.

Gopher gurgles and squeaks behind her mask, then she charges up the steps behind them. She's incredibly fast for someone who isn't able to see. Her long spider legs leap three steps at a time, quickly catching up. She slashes at Rachel's bare back with her jagged blade and the college girl screams.

Conner grabs his sister and kicks the deranged woman in

her muscled stomach. It doesn't hurt her, but it knocks her off balance enough to get his sister out of harm's way. He gets between them and pushes Rachel up the steps.

"Keep going!" he yells.

But she's already picking up the pace, passing Blaise and rushing out of the stairwell to the main deck.

⚓

They find themselves in the main ballroom, filled with empty tables and a stage in the front of the room that must have been used for live bands and comedy acts.

Blaise grabs a chair from the ground and puts it in front of the door, hoping to hold back the strange mutant woman. When Gopher arrives, she slams against the door, squealing and gurgling. But she can't get through.

When Conner and Rachel realize they are safe, they kneel over, trying to catch their breath.

"What the hell was that thing?" Rachel asks.

Blaise shakes his head. "No fucking clue."

"You called her Gopher," Conner says.

Blaise nods. "Gopher was a character from *The Love Boat*. If this ship is *The Pacific Princess*, maybe she's cosplaying as a character from the show."

Conner doesn't believe it. "How is that cosplaying? She just has a picture of a character stuck to her face. She's not even dressed like him."

"Don't ask me," Blaise says.

As they move toward the bar of the ship, they notice that it's still fully stocked. All kinds of bottles of liquor and wine are fully intact.

"Anyone want a drink?" Blaise asks.

Conner says, "Fuck yes. Anything strong."

The woman is still banging on the door, trying to force it

open. The chair isn't going to last forever.

"We don't have time for that," Rachel says. "We need to get out of here. We should get to Addy and Lily before something happens to them."

When she says this, the two men agree. It's no time for a drink, even if the thought of taking the edge off appeals to them.

But before Blaise leaves the side of the bar, a figure stands up from behind the counter. A large muscled man close to seven feet high towers over them, polishing a glass with a rag. He's got the body of a professional wrestler, wearing leather straps across his chest. Fishing hooks are pierced through his ribs and nipples. Small airplane bottles of liquor impale the sides of his neck and shoulders. A metal plate is nailed to his face just like the woman, but this time there's the face of a smiling black man with an afro and a handlebar mustache.

"Isaac Washington…" Blaise says, stepping back.

"Who?" Conner asks.

"He's the bartender from *The Love Boat*."

They look at the large man with the Isaac Washington face.

But Conner is more confused by why the man is white when he's trying to portray a black man.

"Dude, that's cultural appropriation," Conner tells the bartender. "Not cool. That's the same as blackface."

But Isaac Washington doesn't respond. He just keeps washing the pint glass with that big stupid smile radiating at them from the photograph on his face. The man is an intimidating figure and none of them want to get too close to him, but he's not especially violent. He just faces them, as though asking if they want a drink.

The three of them back away. They turn around and head out of the ballroom, trying to figure out how to get back to the medbay.

The three scared people scan the deck, looking for signs to direct them toward the medbay, but they don't find anything. They're lost. The sound of a door smashing open echoes in the distance. They know the woman with the Gopher mask will be coming for them soon. So they just run, not knowing where they're going. They charge toward the swimming pool deck, scanning their surroundings.

"The atrium should be nearby," Blaise says. "We can get to the medbay from there."

But before they get their bearings, two more mutants find them. On the other side of the pool, a large man in a captain's uniform stands there, glaring at them. He is covered in human body parts that have been sewn to his uniform. Severed arms and legs are attached to his chest and waist like straps. He holds a massive cleaver in his hand. The face of Captain Stubing, the star of *The Love Boat*, is nailed to the man's head.

On the other side of the pool, there stands a woman. She has a scarred, sliced up bald scalp with a picture of Julie, the cruise director, nailed to her face. She is topless with breasts that have been sliced and quartered, spread out like two meaty flowers across her chest. A meat hook dangles from one hand and a trident is firmly gripped in the other.

"What the fuck is going on?" Rachel cries. "Who the fuck are these people?"

Before they have time to react, Gopher comes up behind them, brandishing her blades and gurgling in their direction.

"This is so fucked up..." Conner says. He turns to Blaise. "What the hell have you gotten us into?"

Blaise whines, "I didn't do this! These people have nothing to do with me."

But Conner can't believe it. Since Blaise is such a big fan of *The Love Boat* and is the reason they got stranded at sea, Conner can't help but blame him for everything. If only they didn't go on the ship with him none of this would have happened.

"What do we do?" Rachel asks, trying to get them to focus. "We're surrounded."

Blaise looks around, trying to see if there's anywhere they can go.

"We've got two options," Conner says. He looks over them with a confident expression. "We either jump overboard or fight our way past them. My vote is for the latter."

"But we're unarmed," Rachel says. "There's no way we can fight these guys."

Blaise agrees. "It's three on three. If only we had weapons we'd be even."

Rachel shakes her head. "Look at them. Even if we were armed and they weren't, we'd still be at a disadvantage. They look like they have monstrous strength."

"They're also blind," Conner says. "They can't see anything through their masks. We have the advantage."

Rachel looks at their enemy. She knows they can't take them on three-on-three, but she realizes that they're spread apart pretty far. She wonders if they can take them three-on-one.

Conner is thinking the same thing as his sister.

"Let's all go for the captain," he says. "He's the oldest and he's the closest one to an exit."

"How do you expect us to get past him?" Blaise asks.

"The three of us just tackle him," Conner explains. "We shove him to the ground and take his weapon and then bash his head in. We'll be gone before the two women can reach us."

Blaise and Rachel don't like it. Too many things can go wrong. Besides, none of them but Conner is athletic. They won't stand a chance.

"Trust me," Conner says, looking back at them. "I'll take the lead. I'll use my football skills and lay the old guy out. You focus on grabbing his weapon."

Blaise takes a deep breath. "If you think you can take him down I'll follow you."

But Rachel isn't convinced. "There's no fucking way. Conner, don't do it. We should just jump off the side of the ship."

"I'm not leaving my daughter," Blaise says.

"And I'm not leaving my girlfriend," Rachel says. "But we can swim back on board and get to them without having to fight for our lives."

"We're already fighting for our lives," Blaise says, taking his sunglasses out of his pocket and putting them over his eyes. "We might as well try to take one of them out."

Rachel groans. She can't believe she's got to deal with these idiots. But there's nothing that's going to stop them. At least she knows that if things go bad enough she can always jump off the boat as a backup plan. She just hopes nothing will happen before that. She doesn't want to see her brother get hurt.

But when they put their plan into action, they all get ready and charge at Captain Stubing, yelling like Vikings on a warpath, Rachel wishes they would have just gone straight to Plan B.

⚓

Conner comes five feet from Captain Stubing, ready to tackle him to the ground and beat the shit out of him, when his personality changes and he loses consciousness. The new version of Conner has no idea what the hell is going on. He notices that he's yelling and charging at some kind of deformed freak with his sister and some douchey-looking guy running behind him, but he has no idea why they are doing this or what they are trying to accomplish. He wonders if they're on a movie set and acting in some strange pirate movie. He wonders if he's doing a good job or if he should ask the director to let them take a break. But when he looks around, he doesn't see any sign of a director. It's almost as if all of this is real. Not sure what he should do, he decides to just go with it like he always does. He decides he should just run at the deformed man in the captain's uniform and hope for the best.

But because he hesitated and stopped running at his full speed, Captain Stubing has time to react. The deformed captain moves out of Conner's path and then lowers his massive meat cleaver into his chest. The cleaver cuts through Conner's shoulder, bisecting his ribcage and ending in his belly.

Rachel cries and falls back as she sees her brother has been nearly split into two.

"Oh, fuck!" Blaise yells.

Conner looks back at his sister, still not sure what the hell is going on. Then he goes limp. His body falls overboard and plunges into the ocean.

"Conner!" Rachel yells.

She doesn't hesitate. She jumps over the railing and follows her brother into the sea. When Blaise sees that he's all alone with three freakish maniacs, he doesn't know what else to do. Captain Stubing faces him with his massive meat cleaver, ready to cut him in half like he did the college boy. Blaise backs up a few feet and turns around, coming face-to-face with the woman in the Gopher mask. Then he crawls over the railing and jumps overboard before they're able to eviscerate him.

CHAPTER FOUR
ADDY

⚓

Addy wonders why the others are taking so long to get back. It's been over an hour and there's been no sign of them. She doesn't like being stuck with Blaise's weird little kid. Even though she's glad the girl seems to be doing well, she isn't enjoying being in her presence. Lily just sits in the hospital bed, sculpting small animals out of a wad of rotting hamburger meat she took out of her pocket. The girl makes dogs and bunnies and all kinds of small animals with the meat. She realizes there's something seriously wrong with the girl.

"Want me to make you something?" Lily asks Addy. "I can make you a turtle. Do you like turtles?"

Addy shakes her head. "You shouldn't be messing with that. It's full of bacteria."

Lily frowns at her like a cartoon character but Addy doesn't fall for her cute routine.

"You'll get an infection if any of that bacteria gets in your wound," Addy says. "Get rid of it."

"But I'm having fun..." Lily says.

"I don't care. You could die. Throw it away."

Lily pouts and ignores the college girl. She refuses to get rid of the raw hamburger meat and forms it into a new creation. When she's done, she holds it up to Addy.

"What's that supposed to be?" Addy asks.

Lily smiles. "It's a swastika."

"Why the hell would you make a swastika?" Addy cries.

"Because you're being a Nazi and don't want me to play with my meat."

Addy freaks out on the girl. She tears the meat swastika from her hand and throws it in the bin by the bed.

"You do not make swastikas out of hamburger meat, you weirdo!" Addy yells. "What the hell is wrong with you?"

The little girl goes quiet, sitting there with greasy hands, angry that her toy has been snatched away from her.

"I'm not a Nazi, you little bitch," Addy says. "I fucking hate Nazis."

⚓

There's a good reason why Addy hates Nazis. This is because her mother was literally a Nazi. She was a prominent member of the Fourth Reich, a secret organization that has existed ever since the end of the Second World War. Addy hated her mother. She was the most despicable, horrible person she's ever known. And she wants to have nothing to do with her for the rest of her life.

Even though Addy has gone by Addy McCoy the majority of her life, her real name is Adolf Hitler McCoy. But she wasn't just named this because her mother was a Nazi. She was given the name because she is actually a clone of Adolf Hitler himself. During the Third Reich, the Nazis saved some of Hitler's DNA. They were preserving it so that some day they could create a perfect clone of Adolf Hitler. When Addy's mother was chosen to be the incubator for the second coming of Hitler, she couldn't have been happier. She planned to give birth to the Fuhrer and raise him to be the perfect dictator, so that he could rule the Nazis once again.

But it didn't work out the way she expected. Addy was born

as a girl, not a boy. And nobody wanted a girl to rule the Fourth Reich. Addy's mother was kicked out of the organization, and she has been taking it out on her daughter ever since, blaming her little girl for not being born a male.

Addy thanks the stars that she's a woman. If she had been a boy her life would have been much different. She would have been forced to become some kind of leader to a bunch of insane madmen who wanted to take over the world.

Just because she has Hitler's DNA, it doesn't mean she's actually Hitler. Even if she was a boy, she still wouldn't have been Hitler. Addy is a clone of Hitler, an identical match of his DNA. But she's more like his twin sister than his clone, even though she was born decades after his death.

Her life has been difficult growing up knowing that she is the clone of the biggest monster of human history. Whenever she learned about the atrocities that were committed during the second world war, about all that hate crimes that have been committed in his name ever since, she's always felt horrible about it. She feels as though she is somehow responsible for it all. Even though she's a completely different person with a completely different personality and history, she still feels guilty. It's like she really is Hitler. A female version of Hitler. And it's been her biggest secret that she's never been able to share with anyone.

She can't imagine how she would be treated if her secret ever came out. She would be bullied and attacked by everyone who meets her. She would never be able to get a job or do anything in the entertainment industry, even though her dream is to become an actress. Who would ever want to have anything to do with the female clone of Adolf Hitler? Even if she's the nicest person in the world it would destroy a company's brand if word ever got out that they had female Adolf Hitler on staff.

And not only would it hurt her career, but it would be devastating to her love life. Who would want to marry Adolf Hitler? Who would want to have children with her, knowing that they would be the direct descendants of Hitler himself? She knows that there are probably some racist skinheads out there who would love the idea of having Hitler's kids, but she doesn't want to have a relationship with somebody like that. She wants to be loved for who she is. She doesn't want to be loved only because she's Hitler.

But more than any of that, the thing that worries her more than anything, is if Rachel ever found out about it. Her relationship with Rachel is the most important thing in the world to her. And she doesn't think her girlfriend would be too happy about dating the reincarnation of the ultimate symbol of hate. Addy hopes that Rachel would still love her for who she is, not who she came from, but she's not willing to risk it. She doesn't want to admit who she really is, even though it would mean so much to her to be with someone who could empathize with the truth that she's had to live with all this time. It would make her happier than anything if she had somebody in her life who could love her completely, even if she is a female clone of Adolf Hitler.

⚓

Addy tries to apologize to Lily for snapping at her and throwing her meat away. She didn't mean to upset the girl. She was just mad that she was called a Nazi. It's not something she's ever been called, so it took her by surprise. Her mother was a Nazi but she never was. She can't handle anyone thinking of her as one.

"Everything will be okay," Addy tells the sulking girl, trying to cheer her up. "Your dad will come back and we'll find a way off this ship. Once we get back home I'll buy you all the raw hamburger you want."

Lily's eyes light up in excitement. "Are you serious? Do you promise?"

"I promise," Addy says, smiling.

She doesn't see the figure coming into the room until it's too late. Lily's smile turns to a look of shock as she sees the monster entering the room. A man in a doctor's outfit, covered with strange surgical tools strapped to his body. The picture of an older man with glasses is nailed to his face. Lily has never seen *The Love Boat*, so she doesn't know that it's a picture of Doc, the ship's doctor on *The Pacific Princess*.

Before Addy knows what the girl is reacting to, Doc pierces a scalpel into her back. She turns around and sees the horrific man in the doorway, smiling at her in the still photograph. Then she falls back, rolling over the bed to the floor.

Lily screams.

Before Addy can do anything to protect the girl, the doctor pulls a hook-shaped blade from his coat and moves in closer. He aims it at the girl's throat, ready to cut her open as though she's a patient on his operating table.

Addy pulls the scalpel out of her back and looks at it. Blood gushes out of her wound and pools on the floor beneath her. She is in too much shock to know what's going on. She doesn't think any of this could possibly be real.

When she gets to her feet, she sees the doctor grabbing Lily by the throat. He is digging into the girl's mouth with a set of tongs with one hand and holding the hooked blade in the other. When he gets hold of the girl's tongue, he pulls it out of her mouth, stretching it twice as far as it should be able to go. Then he lowers the blade into her mouth, trying to cut out her tongue by the root.

Addy lunges at the man, pushing him over. Blood shoots out of Lily's mouth as the blade connects with her lips, but it doesn't sever her tongue. As Addy grabs hold of the doctor, pulling him away from the operating table, she yells, "Run!"

Lily just looks at her in shock for a moment, not sure what to do.

"Get out of here!" Addy yells.

Lily gets to her feet and rushes for the door.

But before Addy can follow her, the doctor hits her in the side of the head, slamming her skull into the wall. She feels her body going limp. Before she can brace for the fall, Addy blacks out. The doctor hovers over her, looking down with his grotesque surgical equipment.

⚓

Addy wakes up moments later. She's being dragged down a hallway by her hair, pulled by the doctor through the ship. The man gurgles and squeals as though cursing her for letting the young girl escape. Addy has no idea what is happening. She goes in and out of consciousness. When the doctor gets to the stairwell, Addy cries out in pain as her spine hits every step on the way down. She descends backwards, upside-down, and isn't able to get back on her feet. She's too weak to resist the crazed doctor as he tugs on her, nearly ripping the hair from her scalp.

"What the fuck, motherfucker," she cries.

But the guy doesn't ease up. He only pulls her faster, slamming her against every step. When they get down into the dungeon, Addy panics. She can't believe such a place exists on the cruise ship. But instead of worrying about her own wellbeing, Addy thinks about what happened to Rachel. She hasn't seen the others for so long. She wonders if this maniac has already gotten to them. She wonders if Rachel is still alive. It doesn't matter what happens to her as long as her girlfriend is okay. She can't stand the idea of anything happening to her.

But when Addy gets a good look around, she doesn't see Rachel anywhere in the dungeon with her. She sees other people being kept in cages, but none of them are the people she came on board with. This thought allows her to relax. She feels happier, even though she's at the mercy of a deranged killer.

Doc lifts Addy up and puts her on a meat hook. The blade

goes through her back and exits out of her belly. She screams out in pain as her weight pushes down on the hook. But no matter what happens to her, she's still happy that Rachel isn't sharing her fate. She can handle being killed by this sick bastard as long as Rachel gets away.

But when the doctor cuts her across the abdomen and her guts spill out on the floor, Addy cries out for mercy. She doesn't want to die. She doesn't want to be in this amount of pain. Doc lifts up her innards and stuffs them into his pants, rubbing them against his erect penis.

Addy can somehow feel every second of it as he jerks himself off with her intestines while she's still alive.

⚓

Rachel swims through the water, searching for her brother. He fell off the ship before her, but he's nowhere to be seen. Deep down, she knows he's dead, but she doesn't want to believe it. He was cut in half. There's no way anyone can survive that. His body is gone. It has sunk to the bottom of the ocean. But she wants to find it. She wants to bring him back home. Even if he's dead, she has no intention of leaving him for the sharks.

"Come on," Blaise says, grabbing her from behind and pulling her toward his yacht.

The Crotch Moistener is still afloat, despite taking on so much water. It won't last for long, but at least they can get to safety for a brief moment.

"Conner!" Rachel yells out. "Conner!"

Blaise just keeps pulling on her. "He's dead. There's nothing you can do."

But she keeps on yelling, refusing to let her brother go. As Blaise works to get the college girl onto the yacht, he looks up at the cruise ship. The crazed people in *Love Boat* masks are standing at the railing, staring down at them, watching them even though they aren't able to see behind those thick metal plates. As Rachel calls out for her brother, the maniacs cock their heads, listening, trying to pinpoint her exact location through the sound of waves crashing against the side of the ship.

The yacht has taken on a lot of water. The lower deck is mostly underwater and the front of the ship is almost submerged. The boat is at such a steep angle that Rachel and Blaise aren't able to stand upright as they get on board. They crawl across the deck to get what they're after. Rachel goes for her tennis shoes while Blaise gets his speargun that's now caught on the railing, inches away from falling off the ship. When he has his weapon, Blaise goes to his cabinet full of diving gear and retrieves three extra spears. He loads one of them and holds the other two against the side of the barrel.

When he looks up at the top deck of the cruise ship, Blaise doesn't see the freaks anymore. He thinks they must be coming after them, finding hiding spots in order to ambush them the second they go back on board.

"Come on," Blaise says, leading Rachel to the side of his yacht.

He lowers the dinghy into the water and climbs on board, helping Rachel down.

"Where are we going?" Rachel asks. "We're not leaving the others are we?"

Blaise shakes his head. "I'm not ditching my daughter. We have to get her off of there before anything happens to her."

"Then where the hell are we going?" Rachel asks as Blaise paddles the small boat away from the yacht.

Blaise keeps paddling as he explains, "They know we're here. We have to enter from another side of the ship."

"Are we going to be able to find our way back to the medbay?"

"We have to," Blaise says. "And we have to hurry. There's no telling how long they'll be safe in there."

"If they haven't been discovered already..." Rachel says.

Addy writhes in pain as the doctor masturbates with a handful of her intestines. She grips the end of the meat hook, trying to pull herself free. But she doesn't have the strength. She pulls on the chain that holds her off the ground, trying to climb it, make it easier to get the hook out. But it's hopeless. She can't escape on her own.

The act of Addy trying to escape seems to turn the deranged man on even more. Hearing her writhe and whimper in a desperate attempt to free herself makes the doctor giggle and drool beneath his mask, jerking himself off in a fury.

Addy tries kicking at the man, but moving her legs sends lightning shocks of insufferable pain throughout her entire body. Her strikes just barely nudge him and only make him more excited.

"Get the fuck away from me, you sick fuck," she yells, coughing on blood between every word.

The doctor giggles. He pulls a chair to them and stands on it so they can be face to face. Then he unzips his fly and sticks his deformed penis into the cut he made in her abdomen. Addy screams as he fucks her. She can feel his weird bulbous member in her guts as he slides it in and out of her lower entrails. Then he grabs a rope of intestine dangling out of her and puts it in his mouth, sucking on it. He gulps it down, deep-throating her bowels like they are some kind of long fleshy penises.

Addy can't take it anymore. She closes her eyes and looks away, trying to block out the experience. She has no idea why she's still alive. Having her guts ripped out like this should have been enough to end her life. She wants it to end. She wants to die. But no matter what the sick man does to her, death won't come.

"Just kill me already!" Addy cries.

But the doctor doesn't stop. He refuses to end her life. While

Addy prays to have her life taken away, the doctor fucks her open cavity, smearing his penis with her guts until he ejaculates inside of her. She can feel his warm fluid squirting against her entrails, oozing down her innards toward her bladder and kidneys.

As the doctor grunts and groans, holding them together for a moment, wheezing behind his mask, Addy wonders if she doesn't deserve all of this. She's the clone of Adolf Hitler. If anyone deserves to suffer like she is, it would be the man who was responsible for The Holocaust. So many people endured such horrific atrocities because of him. And it's like the universe wants her to suffer in his stead. Nobody in the world would feel bad for her if they knew what she was. Everyone would think this treatment was perfectly justified. Because she has Hitler's DNA, all of this is defensible. She deserves the worst death that anyone could give her.

Addy opens her eyes and looks at the picture of the smiling middle-aged doctor in front of her, the face of a lovable character from a 1970s sitcom. The image is scarred into her brain. Such a nice, friendly face is doing such a horrible thing to her. It's her fault. He would never do anything so cruel unless she deserved it. It's all her fault.

Then the doctor rips off Addy's pants and proceeds to fuck her with her own intestines.

⚓

Rachel puts on her tennis shoes and knots them tight. She can't believe she's stuck wearing the stupid sailor-themed bikini that Blaise bought her. If only she took it off before Blaise threw her luggage overboard, she wouldn't have to deal with having her ass hanging out in a life or death scenario. The sun is high in the sky, burning her pale skin. She doesn't even have suntan lotion. She's feeling dehydrated and needs to sleep. If she doesn't get under cover soon she's going to have a heatstroke.

Blaise pulls up to the gangway on the other side of the ship, rowing right below the bottom step. He picks Rachel up on his shoulders and lifts her up so that she can reach. Once she grabs hold and pulls herself up, Blaise tosses up a rope so that she can tie the dinghy to it.

Despite his weight, Rachel is able to help pull him up to the gangway. She lifts him until he can reach the bottom step. Then he climbs the rest of the way up on his own.

"Damn, girl," Blaise says. "When did you get so strong?"

"I've been working out," Rachel says.

Even though she says this, Rachel hasn't actually been working out. In fact, she's been working out less than she ever has in her life. She's not sure exactly why, but ever since she infected herself with the strange parasites she bought off of the black market, she's become a lot stronger than she used to be. It's like the parasites crawling under her skin are building up her muscles to be tight and burly, to make them better nests to lay their eggs in. She doesn't appear more muscular. She looks just as soft as she did when she used to ditch class and lie in bed watching movies and eating chocolates all day. But she's definitely stronger. She could probably lift Blaise up over her head as easily as lifting a pillow.

"Let's go," Blaise says. "Move as quietly as you can. I don't think they can see. As long as we keep quiet, they won't be able to find us."

Rachel agrees.

They move up the gangway as stealthily as they can. When they get up to the atrium, they see the cruise director stalking the lobby like a feral animal. Listening for movement, her head cocking to one side. Blaise holds Rachel back, putting his finger to his mouth to quiet her.

The woman with the Julie mask gurgles and wheezes, holding up the hook she uses for a hand, ready to strike at anything she hears.

Blaise creeps up behind the woman and aims his speargun at her. He sits there for a moment, not making a sound, not even breathing. He waits for the woman to stop moving and then pulls the trigger.

The spear shoots out and impales the woman in the back. She topples to the ground.

"Yes!" Blaise yells, but then he realizes the volume of his voice and goes back to a whisper. "Got the bitch."

Rachel comes up behind him and they approach the freakish woman. They stand over her body. She smells terrible. She's covered in grime that must be a combination of feces, vomit and dried blood. It's like the woman got off on smearing human fluids over her naked body, no matter how rancid and disgusting they were.

"Let's keep going," Rachel says in a soft tone.

Blaise agrees. He pulls the spear out of the dead mutant and puts a new one in the gun. Then they continue on toward the medbay.

⚓

When Blaise and Rachel arrive in the doctor's office, they find the room is covered in blood. It looks like a struggle took place. Lily and Addy are nowhere in sight.

"Fucking hell..." Rachel says. "We're too late."

Blaise becomes furious. "Motherfuckers... They better not have laid a hand on my daughter."

Rachel looks around the room, trying to find a clue as to what happened there. Outside of the blood, there's no telling what occurred. They don't even know whose blood it is.

"We need to look for them," Rachel says.

Blaise agrees.

When they leave the medbay and go back up to the lobby, they realize that the body of the cruise director is nowhere in sight. There's a puddle of blood on the floor where the freak wearing the Julie mask was lying. But she's gone.

"What do you think happened?" Rachel asks. "Did she just get up and walk away or did somebody drag her off?"

Blaise shakes his head. "She wasn't dragged."

He points at some bloody footprints leading off toward the pool deck.

"How did she walk away from that?" Rachel asks. "She was dead. I'm sure of it."

"I didn't check her pulse."

"But that spear went right through the back of her heart," Rachel says. "There's no way anyone would survive that."

Blaise doesn't know how to explain it. He turns his eyes away from the blood and scans the area.

"We need to find Lily and get the hell out of here," he says.

"*And* Addy," Rachel says. "Don't forget her."

Blaise nods. "Yeah, and her too. We're not leaving this ship until we find them. Dead or alive."

Rachel retrieves the food and water they took from the yacht and they head off to find their missing loved ones.

⚓

Lily tried running and hiding for a while. She found a passenger cabin and was able to lock herself in, but she quickly became bored. Lily hates being bored. She'd rather get stabbed in the back and dragged off by a deranged doctor then spend another minute hiding in that room.

So Lily decides to explore. She sees a topless woman with weird flower-shaped boobs wandering the hallway, gripping a wound on her chest with a hook-shaped hand and carrying a trident in the other. Lily decides it would be best not to bother her so she sneaks away.

She arrives in a vast ballroom, one that must have been used for dancing and musical acts at one point, but it's completely empty now. Lily goes to the bar and climbs up into a stool.

A big smile grows on her face as she spins around in the stool. Then she says, "Bartender, I would like a scotch on the rocks."

She nearly falls back when a large man stands up from behind the bar. He towers over her, flexing his massive muscles. There's a picture of a friendly, smiling black man with a handlebar mustache looking back at her. Before she has a chance to react, the bartender pours her a drink in a lowball glass and passes it to her. She looks down at the glass of scotch and frowns.

"Actually, can I have a Shirley Temple?" Lily asks him.

The bartender nods and makes her a new drink. There isn't any ice, but he is able to pour her a ginger ale with grenadine and a maraschino cherry on top. When Lily gets the drink, she takes a sip and cringes. The ginger ale is flat. The cherry is old and dry. But she smiles anyway and takes another sip.

"You wouldn't happen to have any raw meat, would you?" Lily asks the bartender.

The large man nods. He goes behind the counter grabs a large chunk of meat with a hook and plops it down on the counter in front of her. When Lily looks at it, she seems disappointed. It's a piece of a human thigh, still on the bone.

"Hmmm..." she says. "I guess it's better than nothing."

Lily puts her hands on the meat and squeezes it, squishing it with her fingers. But it's very firm. It doesn't mold very well. It's also very old and rancid. It smells terrible. Lily is accustomed to the smell of rotten meat, but she hates when it's so tough and rigid.

"Do you have a meat grinder by any chance?" Lily asks him. "I want to make a sculpture but this meat is too hard to mold. I don't like it."

The bartender is confused about what to do. He doesn't appear to have a meat grinder handy. He searches under the bar with his hands, feeling around to find something that might work. Then he pulls out a cheese grater and holds it up to the girl.

"A cheese grater?" Lily asks.

The man with the Isaac Washington mask picks up the chunk of thigh meat and rubs it against the cheese grater. He uses his massive amount of strength to shred the meat as easily as a block of cheese.

When the shredded meat piles up on the counter, Lily's eyes light up in excitement.

"Oh, wow!" she cries. "I didn't know you could do that with a cheese grater!"

Once half the thigh is in a pile of shreds on the counter, Lily grabs it by the handful and creates a mound in front of her. Then she digs her fingers in and squeezes. The texture is amazing. She's never felt anything like it before.

"This is perfect!" she tells the bartender. "Thank you so much!"

The bartender nods his head and puts the cheese grater down. Then he straightens his back, waiting for the next customer.

Lily molds the meat into a ball and then stretches it out, kneading it like dough.

"I'll make you a swan," Lily says. "Do you like swans?"

The bartender shakes his head.

"What about ducks?" Lily asks.

The bartender shakes his head again.

"Are you sure?" Lily asks. "I'm really good at making ducks."

The bartender thinks about it for a minute. Then he shrugs and nods his head.

"Good," Lily tells him, beginning her creation. "I'll make you the best meat duck you've ever seen."

The bartender can't help but get excited for the end result.

⚓

When Rachel and Blaise finally find Lily, they are shocked to see her sitting at the bar, chatting with the hulk of man wearing the Isaac Washington mask. Lily is holding up what looks like a duck made of meat, handing it to the bartender. The large man takes the duck in his hands and feels it, exploring the shape with his fingers. Then he nods in approval and hands it back to the girl.

Blaise yells at his daughter, "Get away from him, baby girl! He's dangerous!"

When Lily notices her father is in the room with her, she rolls her eyes, annoyed that he interrupted her yet again while she's finally able to play with some meat.

"Don't be so melodramatic, Dad," Lily tells him.

Blaise aims his speargun at the bartender as he steps closer, ready to take him out the second he breathes wrong.

"Calmly move away from him," Blaise says.

Lily cringes at her dad. "Eww… you're so annoying."

Then she goes back to molding a new shape in her wad of flesh.

Blaise is losing patience with his daughter. "Come on, Lily. It's time to go."

He reaches out to her, not taking his eyes off of Isaac Washington. When he gets close enough, he grabs her by the shoulder and pulls her off the stool.

"Run!" Blaise yells.

Lily fights him. "Let me go, you asshole!"

Then Blaise fires his speargun, shooting the bartender in the chest.

"Let's get out of here!" Blaise yells.

When Lily sees the spear in the bartender's chest, her eyes fill with shock.

"Why did you do that?" Lily cries. "He's my friend!"

Isaac Washington roars in anger. He tears the spear out of his chest and lunges over the bar.

"Run!" Blaise yells.

The three of them flee into the stairwell, heading back to the dinghy. The large man's angry screams are muffled behind his mask as he charges after them. But he doesn't follow them after they leave the ballroom, as though he's unwilling to leave his post behind the bar.

⚓

They realize they're safe once they get back to the gangway leading down to the dinghy. They pause to catch their breath. Lily is whining and punching at her dad to let her go, annoyed that he interfered with her fun.

When the girl calms down, Rachel bends down to her and asks, "What happened to you? Where's Addy?"

Lily frowns, still annoyed about being taken away while she was playing with meat. She glares at Rachel as though it's just as much her fault as it was her dad's.

"I need you to tell me what happened to her," Rachel says.

Lily shrugs. "She was taken by the doctor."

Rachel doesn't know what that means but it still fills her with worry. "What doctor?"

Lily shrugs again. "I don't know, some weirdo in a mask and a doctor's outfit. He stabbed her and then took her away."

When the girl says this, Rachel's heart sinks in her chest. She's terrified about what happened to her girlfriend.

Rachel grabs Lily by the shoulders. "Where is she? Where was she taken?"

Lily wiggles out of her grip. "I saw him take her downstairs, but I didn't follow them. That doctor was a total jerk. He tried to cut my tongue out."

When Blaise hears this, he goes to Lily and squeezes her

cheeks, looking into her mouth. "Are you okay? Did he hurt you?"

Lily pulls away. "He cut me a little, but I'm fine."

"We need to get out of here," Blaise says, holding his daughter by the hand. "Let's go before another one of them comes."

"What about Addy?" Rachel asks.

"What about her?" Blaise says.

"We still need to find her. If she was taken downstairs she's probably in the dungeon where all those freaks were being kept prisoner."

Blaise shakes his head. "I'm not going down there. We need to go."

"You said we wouldn't leave without Addy and Lily," Rachel says.

Blaise points at her. "Your friend is obviously dead. Just let her go. We can still save ourselves if we leave now."

Rachel shakes her head. "I'm not leaving without her."

"Then we're leaving without you," Blaise says.

"Are you fucking serious?"

Blaise holds up his hand. "What do you expect me to do? I can't risk my daughter's life for your friend who's already been stabbed."

Rachel thinks about it for a minute. She knows it's a long shot that Addy is still alive, but she can't just leave without knowing for sure. But she also understands that Blaise wouldn't want to risk his daughter's life. She can't ask him to do that for her friend's sake, even though he's a horrific asshole and his daughter's a little creep.

"Tell you what..." Rachel begins. "How about you take the dinghy and get away from the ship, but don't leave the area for another twenty minutes? Stay at a safe distance. Once I find Addy, we'll jump overboard and you can come pick us up." She looks Blaise in the eyes. "Is that fair?"

Blaise takes a breath and then nods his head. "Okay. But

just twenty minutes. Not a second more."

Rachel grips him by the shoulder, staring him in the eyes to thank him for giving her this opportunity, even though she rejected his marriage proposal and made him feel like a jerk. When they're ready to part, Rachel hands him the supplies and then heads back up the stairs. Blaise and Lily climb their way down to the dinghy.

"See you soon," Rachel calls down to him.

Blaise nods. "Yeah, whatever."

⚓

Blaise has no intention of waiting around for her. That bitch deserves it for rejecting him and saying all those mean things about him. Daddy Cool doesn't deserve that kind of abuse. Besides, they don't have enough food and water for four people to survive at sea for long. Blaise has no choice but to leave Rachel behind. His daughter's life depends on it.

As Blaise raises the sail on the dinghy and heads out to sea, leaving the cruise ship behind them, Lily becomes upset.

"Hey!" she cries. "You said you'd wait twenty minutes for her."

Blaise shrugs. "I gave her a chance to come with us. But she had to be a stubborn bitch."

"You're such an asshole!"

Blaise doesn't let her words bother him. "I'm doing it for you, baby girl. I'm saving your life."

"No, you're saving yourself."

"Daddy Cool knows what's best for both of us."

"You're such a piece of shit."

Blaise doesn't care what she says to him. He knows he made the most responsible decision as a father. Sometimes you have to be a complete selfish asshole in order to do what's best for your children.

⚓

Rachel doesn't realize she's been ditched until she goes to the opposite side of the ship, heading for the stairwell down to the dungeon. She takes a peek over the railing, curious to see if the yacht is still afloat, but what she sees is that Blaise has betrayed her. The dinghy has sailed around to the front of the ship and is heading back in the direction of the coast, leaving Rachel and her girlfriend behind.

"You son of a bitch!" Rachel yells.

She moves to the top deck to get a better look, to make sure it's true. But there's no doubt about it. The asshole is going as fast as he can to get the hell out of there and save himself. He couldn't even wait twenty minutes for her. She's so mad that she could kill him.

"I hope you fucking sink, you asshole!" Rachel yells.

But then she realizes she's attracting too much attention to herself. Before she knows it, the woman with elongated breasts and the Gopher mask comes up behind her, scratching her blades together and gurgling in anticipation.

When Rachel turns to see the deranged woman's wiry body, hovering over her like a scarecrow, Rachel panics. She jumps over the railing and lands on the gangway leading to the yacht. But once she's there, she realizes there's nowhere left to go. She goes down the steps toward *The Crotch Moistener*, but Blaise's ship is already underwater. The chain that held it to the gangway has snapped and the vessel is probably at the bottom of the sea.

Rachel looks up at the picture of Gopher, staring down at her with his handsome 1970s smile. She doesn't know what to do. If she jumps overboard she'll never be able to get back onto the ship. She'll never be able to find Addy.

There's no other choice. She has to fight her way through the deranged woman. The only thing Rachel thinks that she can use as a weapon is the yacht's anchor that is still attached to the gangway. She goes to it and lifts it up. The anchor is over thirty pounds and was too heavy for the men to handle, but when Rachel picks it up it feels incredibly light. Not much heavier than a baseball bat. The parasites in her body really have done something to change her muscles. She's never felt so strong before.

As Gopher comes down at her with a jagged blade in each hand, Rachel just stands there, waiting, holding up the anchor like a baseball bat. The college girl tries to stay as still as possible, trying not to make a sound. If the crazy woman really can't see through that mask, she won't see her attack coming.

With Rachel's strength, she'll be able to break open this freak's skull easier than a rotten pumpkin. All the freak has to do is come in close enough and Rachel will end her. She will smash this freak to pieces and toss her corpse overboard.

But once Gopher comes into range and Rachel swings the anchor, the mutant jumps out of the way as though she was able to feel the shift in the air. Gopher twists around the makeshift weapon, bending in an inhuman way. She curls around the anchor and slams Rachel against the side of the ship with her elbow. Then she drives the blade of her knife into the back of the college girl's neck.

Rachel backs away, warm fluid leaking down her back. She can feel the knife still inside her, going deep into her collarbone. Her strength leaves her. She drops the anchor and falls down the steps, rolling backwards like a ragdoll, leaving thick splatters of blood all the way down.

⚓

When the doctor is done with Addy, he pulls her naked, beaten body off of the meat hook and then carries her to the cells with the other prisoners. He unlocks a cage three cells down and tosses her inside, throwing her into a pile of wriggling shit-covered bodies. Then he shuts and locks the door, leaving her with her new friends.

Addy doesn't move until she hears the footsteps fade away and is positive the monster is gone.

"What the fuck…" Addy cries, too weak to move.

She looks down at her abdomen to see the bundle of intestines dangling out of her stomach. She doesn't know why she's still alive, but she prays that it will all be over soon. She begs for her suffering to finally end.

Addy lets her breath leave her lungs, closing her eyes, imagining her life slip away. But nothing happens. She keeps on living. Her pain only gets worse.

Then something moves beneath her. The pile of bodies she's lying on aren't corpses. They wake up, writhing and moaning.

Addy's eyes shoot open.

"What the fuck!"

She tries to climb down, but filthy bony limbs reach out and grab her. She looks down at the people. There's no way that any of them can still be alive. They have sliced throats and torn open bellies. Several of them have their eyeballs gouged out or their tongues cut off. One of them crawls out from beneath the others, exposing a cut open chest. His lungs and heart have been removed. Another one is missing the top of her skull and there are several penis-shaped holes in her brain. These creatures can't be alive. They are like zombies.

Addy tries to crawl away, but they just grab her, pulling her toward them. Then they pile on top of her, holding her down. They lick and kiss and bite her flesh. They rub their shriveled penises on her, pushing their feces-coated breasts in her mouth.

Her eyes go wide and she tries to scream, but she doesn't have the strength to resist, her cries muffled within the pit of soiled flesh. The mass of skeletal mutants have their way with her and she closes her eyes tight, trying to block it all out.

She realizes that she must be in hell. There's no other

possibility. She's damned to an eternity of torment, all because of the person who shares the same DNA as she does. His victims have come for her and they plan to make her pay for everything that she hasn't even done.

CHAPTER FIVE
DADDY COOL

⚓

Blaise is sailing out to sea, trying to get as far away from the hellish cruise ship as fast as he can. But for as long as they travel, Blaise can't seem to leave the boat full of monsters behind him. It's like the ship is following them. He doesn't know how it's possible. The ship was adrift. It wasn't operational. But the massive vessel continues on their tail. He tries to pick up the pace, using his basic sailing knowledge to get the tiny vessel to move faster.

"God damn it," Blaise yells, looking back. "What the fuck?"

Lily doesn't share his concern. She just glares at him with a look of disgust on her face.

"I can't believe you'd just leave your girlfriend like that," Lily says to him.

Blaise groans at her. "She's not my girlfriend anymore."

"Still. It's a total dick move."

"I thought you hated Rachel," Blaise says.

"I do, but even I wouldn't do something so shitty."

"When did you start swearing so much?" Blaise asks. "You sound as trashy as your mother."

"I do not!" Lily cries. She hates when he compares her to her mother. There's no one in the world she'd rather be less like than that selfish bitch. Even Blaise is preferable to her. The only good thing about her mother is that she doesn't crave attention like her father does. As long as Lily does what's expected of her, her mother leaves her alone.

"Just let me focus on getting us home," Blaise says, turning back to the ship behind them. "We can probably get back in a couple days if we're lucky."

"A couple of days?" Lily whines.

Blaise nods. "At least we'll be able to get home at all."

⚓

When they finally get far enough away from the cruise ship, Blaise is able to relax. It won't be long before they lose the crazed mutants entirely and can just focus on getting back home. There is an emergency beacon on board the dinghy but Blaise doesn't want to use it, just in case *The Pacific Princess* is able to track them.

"I think we're safe now, baby girl," he says to her. "Daddy Cool pulled through for you."

Lily groans and rolls her eyes. Then she asks him a serious question. "You've never explained it to me before. Why do you always insist on being called Daddy Cool?"

Blaise smiles. "You know, because I'm a dad. And I'm cool."

Lily laughs. "You're not cool."

"Of course I'm cool. How can I not be cool?"

"*No* dads are cool. Daddy Cool is an oxymoron."

Blaise laughs at her words. "It's not an oxymoron. Most dads aren't cool, but I'm an exception. You never got to meet my father, but *he* was a dad who wasn't cool. He was the most uncool dad I've ever met."

Lily shakes her head. "Serious. Why are you so obsessed with that nickname? You've been calling yourself that my whole life."

Blaise loses the smile from his face and lowers his eyes. "Maybe I'll tell you when you're older."

"I'm old enough now." Lily touches the bandages on her chest. "You nearly killed me today. You owe me at least that."

Blaise lets out a sigh.

"Fine…" he says. "But you have to promise not to hate me if I tell you."

"I already hate you now," Lily says.

"Fair enough." Blaise chuckles and then his voice goes soft as he explains. "I never wanted to be a father. The idea of having children used to disgust me. I always thought it would be the worst thing that could ever happen to me."

"Gee thanks," Lily says.

Blaise holds up his hands. "I told you that you might hate me. That's why I didn't want to explain."

Lily lets him off the hook. "Whatever… keep going."

Blaise continues, "When your mother was pregnant with you, I was furious. I was ready to leave her. The bitch didn't even tell me until it was too late to have an abortion."

Lily gets a little offended. "Serious, Dad?"

"Hey, I'm being honest with you," Blaise says. "You would've been aborted in a second if she wasn't delusional about wanting to have a child, a decision she regretted almost immediately after you were born."

"What does any of this have to do with you being called Daddy Cool?"

"Everything," Blaise says. "I didn't want to be a father but the only thing worse than being a father was if I became a bad father. I didn't want to be like my own dad. I didn't want to be a shitty parent. I wanted to be a cool father, the kind of dad kids would love to have around."

"So you wanted to be Daddy Cool?"

Blaise shakes his head. "No, I just wanted to forget the fact that I hate being a father. Calling myself Daddy Cool is how I trick myself into thinking that I'm proud of being a parent rather than disgusted by it. Daddy Cool is the person I want to be. He's a man who loves his kids and cares about their happiness. But Blaise is an asshole. Blaise is just looking for an excuse to ditch his kids and whore wife and go live a carefree life far away from you all. Every time you kids call me Daddy Cool, it kills those selfish thoughts. It's what keeps me going."

Lily is touched by his honesty, but she's not buying it. "Then why do you have your girlfriend call you Daddy Cool?"

Blaise immediately dodges the question. "Look, it doesn't matter who calls me Daddy Cool. As long as I see myself as Daddy Cool, it makes me a better person. That's why I do it."

Lily shakes her head. "Fine, I get it."

Blaise pauses for a moment, waiting for his daughter's eyes to meet his.

"So you'll start calling me Daddy Cool?" he asks.

Lily groans. "No way! I hate calling you Daddy Cool."

Blaise smiles. "Come on, I just told you what it means to me."

"You just told me that you despise being my father," she says. "Why would I reward you for that?"

"Come on," Blaise says. "Call me Daddy Cool."

Lily shakes her head. "Absolutely not."

He leans in close. "Daddy who?"

"No way. I'm not doing it."

He raises his eyebrows at her. "Daddy who?"

Lily sighs. "Fine. Just this once. Daddy…"

Before she can say it, Lily starts hemorrhaging. Her wound has broken open and blood is gushing down her chest, leaking out of her mouth.

"Lily!" he cries.

Her eyes roll back and she spasms, as though she can't breathe. Blaise lowers the sails and goes to his daughter.

"What's wrong?" Blaise asks. "What the hell's happening?"

She was fine just a minute ago. Blaise doesn't understand why her condition is worsening so quickly. He wonders if she was just running on adrenalin this whole time and now that they're finally a good distance from *The Pacific Princess* and beginning to feel safe, her real condition is coming through.

"Don't die, baby girl," Blaise says, tears forming in his eyes. "Please don't die. I can't live without you."

He tries to stop her bleeding, pressing his hands tightly to her chest. But he doesn't know what to do. He doesn't know how to save her.

"I love you so much," he says.

Blaise doesn't think there's anything he can do to help. He's losing her and there's nothing he can do.

"You mean everything to me…"

He hates himself for being such a shitty father. He wishes it was him instead of her. He wishes he could make everything better.

He doesn't realize that he hasn't called himself Daddy Cool even once.

⚓

Before Blaise notices it, the cruise ship catches up to them. It charges through the sea at full speed, as though hunting them down. When he looks up at the vessel, he realizes that it really is seaworthy. It wasn't a derelict. The ship is fully operational. He has no idea how the captain can steer the ship with a metal plate nailed over his eyes, but the monster has somehow managed to reach them.

Blaise has to get moving, but he doesn't want to leave his daughter's side. She doesn't have much longer to live. He'd rather spend that last moment with her even if it means being captured by the vessel of freaks.

Lily opens her eyes and looks up at her father's tears dropping down on her. She doesn't know why he's so upset.

"What's wrong with you?" Lily asks, annoyed that her father's so close.

She seems to be getting better. Blaise has no idea why, but

her bleeding has stopped. She is breathing normally again.

When Lily sits up and notices the cruise ship racing toward them, she panics. "Holy shit! They're coming!"

Then she turns to her father. "What the hell are you doing? Get us out of here!"

Blaise doesn't question her newfound health and goes back to the sails. He gets the dinghy back to full spread and tries to out maneuver the cruise ship. But *The Pacific Princess* is going too fast. They're not going to be able to outrun it.

When the cruise ship gets close enough, the mutants launch something at them. Blaise only sees it for a second. He doesn't have time to pay close attention to what's going on behind him. But then something else is launched. It flies over the dinghy and lands in the water. Blaise gets a good look at the screaming naked man as he plunges into the sea.

"What the fuck is that?" Blaise yells.

"They're throwing people at us!" Lily cries.

Blaise looks back to see two makeshift catapults on the deck of the ship. The mutants are loading them with prisoners from below deck. They are shooting them into the sky like rocks, trying to take out the little dinghy. A shrieking bald man splashes next to the boat, spraying Lily with seawater. As the man gets to the surface, gasping for air, he is reeled back in by a chain connected to his leg. The wardens of the cruise ship have no intention of letting their slaves go. They just want to use them as weapons, not concerned with their safety or wellbeing.

One woman's neck breaks as she slams into the back of the dinghy, putting a crack in the boat. She goes limp in the water before she is reeled back in.

"Why are they doing this?" Lily cries, confused by the violent display.

"Just keep your head down," Blaise tells her.

The next man that is launched from the catapult rips a hole into the sail of the dinghy. Another man goes right through the mast, bending the aluminum pole in half. The tiny vessel is nearly capsized as it is hit by two more half-dead mutants.

"God damn it!" Blaise yells as his boat slows down.

The sails are no longer able to catch the wind. He has to switch to rowing.

He looks at his daughter. She's a tough kid, but even she has a look of distress on her face.

"Don't worry about it, baby girl," he tells her. "We can still get out of this."

Although he rows the dinghy at a slug's pace, he knows that it's not easy for cruise ships to turn around. Instead of trying to outrun them, Blaise paddles away from it. The ship will take at least half an hour to change course and come back for them. Then Blaise can just use that tactic over and over again until they get close enough ashore to flag down somebody for help. Since *The Pacific Princess* doesn't have any small crafts of their own to come after him, Blaise is sure he has the advantage over them.

But there's one problem. The prisoners are still being catapulted at them. And without sails, the dinghy has become a much easier target. One of them is launched at them and grabs hold of the side of the boat. The slobbering man looks more dead than alive. His face has been caved in. His eyes, nose, and mouth have been cut out to expose a fleshy hollow pit. Blaise has no idea how the man is even able to function in such a condition.

Blaise yells at the stowaway and hits him repeatedly with the blunt end of an oar. "Get. The fuck. Off."

But before Blaise can get the freak to let go, Captain Stubing orders his crew to reel them in. Gopher and Isaac Washington pull the chain connected to the prisoner, dragging the dinghy toward the cruise ship.

"They've got us!" Lily yells.

Blaise keeps punching and shoving the freak, but can't get him to let go. He has no idea why this pathetic creature would be helping the ship's crew. This man has been tortured and mutilated by *the Love Boat* monsters. Why would he be on their side? He can only assume that the prisoners have been beaten into complete submission. Or perhaps they have been promised favoritism if they help capture new prey. Whatever the case, Blaise is almost more frightened of the slaves than he is of the slavers.

Since the prisoner holds the side of the boat in a death grip, Blaise isn't able to get free. He has no choice but to point his speargun directly into the freak's sunken face and pull the trigger. The man goes limp and lets go of his grip on the boat. With the dinghy no longer hooked like a fish, Blaise grabs the oars and paddles with all his strength, trying to get out of their range.

Captain Stubing attempts to move the ship in their direction, but the vessel is too massive. It can't catch them. But before Blaise and Lily can get away, the mutants launch two last prisoners at them. One falls too short. But a naked woman with no legs and a bloody skull where her scalp used to be goes far and fast enough to reach the back of the dinghy. Only she doesn't grab the boat. Once she lands in the back of the dinghy, she wraps her arms around Lily. The girl doesn't even have time to scream before she is ripped out of the boat.

"Lily!" Blaise cries, reaching out for his daughter's foot.

But his daughter is out of his reach. She plunges into the sea, sucked under the waves, and *The Pacific Princess* reels her in like a fish.

⚓

Rachel wakes up on the gangway, dangling over the railing. She pulls herself up and gets to her feet, wondering where she is and what the hell happened to her. She feels a sharp object in the back of her neck. When she touches it, she realizes that it's a knife but only barely remembers how it got there. She remembers her fight with Gopher and how she didn't survive the attack. But she's alive now for some reason. She pulls the blade out, feeling it come out from deep in her collarbone and how it tears her muscle fibers wider. Warm blood streams down her back.

She has no idea if she is dead or about to die. Either way, she is standing and able to move around despite the immense amount of pain. There's only one thing on her mind. She has to find Addy. Whether her girlfriend is dead or alive, she wants to spend her last breaths finding her. Maybe she'll be able to save her. Maybe she'll be able to die by her side. Either way, she's not going to give up until she finds out what happened to the only person she's ever truly loved.

Rachel's blood splatters up the steps as she ascends the gangway, leaving a trail of squirming fetus worms. She tosses the crude knife over the railing and retrieves the yacht's anchor, lifting it up over her shoulder. The worms in her body are more active than usual, even though it's the middle of the day. They crawl under her skin like they're going into a feeding frenzy, but the sensation is making Rachel's pain go away, replaced with sexual energy. She feels twice as strong as she was before. The anchor resting on her shoulder feels as light as a claw hammer.

When she gets to the top deck, she sees a row of prisoners being led toward the front of the ship by a madman in a doctor's coat. They are too busy stumbling and moaning to notice her. Up ahead, there are two catapults launching the prisoners into the sea. Three more mutants with face plates of *Love Boat* characters are staring off into the ocean, aiming the catapults at someone in the water. Rachel assumes it is Blaise they are after. They must think she is already dead and aren't concerned with her, so Rachel sneaks past them. She heads into the stairwell leading down into the dungeon.

⚓

When Rachel finds Addy, she can't believe her eyes. Her girlfriend has been torn open, her guts hanging out of her abdomen, covered in blood and feces. Eyeless prisoners are licking and biting her corpse.

"Addy!" Rachel cries, running to the cell.

She reaches her hand into the bars, but can't reach. She slams her anchor into the lock and breaks it off the chain, then pulls open the door.

"Those psychos…" she says.

With the cell ajar, the eyeless prisoners get to their feet and lunge forward. At first it seems like they are rushing for the exit, but they go straight for Rachel. The woman in the sailor bikini swings her anchor at the first man who reaches her. She knocks him to the ground and then drives the anchor down onto his head. She beats him repeatedly until his skull is in pieces on the floor, splattering his brain into a paste, screaming and yelling at him, as though this pathetic creature is solely responsible for her girlfriend's condition. When the other prisoners witness the punishment inflicted on their cellmate, they back away. They fall to their knees and cower in the corner, trying to keep as much distance from the woman as they can. They can tell she's just as dangerous and frightening as the people who have tortured them and imprisoned them there for so long.

Rachel goes to Addy. The girl is still moving. Her guts are spread out across the room, but she's still alive.

"Addy…" Rachel kneels down and curls around the girl, lifting her head and staring down into her flickering eyes. "What did they do to you?"

Addy breathes rapidly, in so much pain that she can barely stay conscious. Rachel can tell she doesn't have much time left. Addy could die at any second. Rachel breaks into tears. Fetus worms leak from the hole in the back of her neck, they slide down her chest and burrow their way into Addy's open cavity.

"No…." Addy moans. "No more…"

Rachel shakes her and calls her name until Addy's eyes finally open. They stare at each other for a moment. A smile curls on Addy's lips.

"You came for me…" Addy says.

Rachel smiles back. "Of course I did. I love you."

"I love you, too." Addy's eyes roll back, but she catches herself. She tries to stay conscious.

"Run…" Addy says. "Get out of here. Save yourself."

"I'm not leaving you," Rachel says.

Addy lifts her hand and caresses Rachel's cheek. "You're so beautiful… I don't deserve anyone as beautiful as you."

Rachel shakes her head. "*I* don't deserve anyone as beautiful as *you*."

"You wouldn't say that if you knew who I really was. I don't deserve love."

"Of course you do!" Rachel says. "I've loved you my whole life. I don't want to be with anyone else. If you die I don't want to live. I'd rather be here with you than anywhere else in this world."

Addy coughs up blood. She doesn't tell Rachel that she's really a clone of the most monstrous dictator in human history. She'd rather die without her knowing. Addy wants to die in her girlfriend's arms, basking in the warmth of her love. She doesn't want to ruin it. She doesn't want her girlfriend to be filled with disgust for her, not during her final moments.

The two of them sit together, holding each other, for what seems like hours. But neither of them die. Their blood and parasites mix together with their tears and sweat and grime. But they are still breathing. Something is keeping them alive.

While being lost inside her thoughts, Rachel can't help but get angry. She loses the desire to just sit there and die in a cell with her girlfriend. She wants those responsible to pay for what they've done. If they just let themselves die like this those mutants will go unpunished. They'll be free to do the same thing to other people like them. Rachel can't allow this to happen. She releases Addy and gets to her feet.

"Who did this to you?" she asks her girlfriend.

Addy looks up at her. "What are you going to do?"

She picks up the bloody anchor and lifts it to her shoulder. "I'm going to destroy them."

Addy shakes her head. "Don't do it. If you can get off this ship and escape I would be happy. But I don't want you to risk your life just to get revenge."

Rachel won't listen to her. She doesn't want to escape. She couldn't live with herself if she left Addy in this state. But if she can kill those responsible, they'll be able to die in peace. Despite her wound, Rachel feels stronger than she's ever been. She feels like an instrument of death.

"It was the doctor," Addy explains. "The one dressed like a doctor is the one who did this to me."

Rachel looks her in the eyes and says, "I'll make him suffer."

Addy nods. She can't help but smile when Rachel says this. She loves the woman so much. Although she doesn't want to see her harmed, she can't help but feel confident that her girlfriend will bring her justice. The idea makes her proud to be with someone so strong and secure, someone who doesn't take shit from anyone.

"Fuck him up for me," Addy says, smiling. "Rip off his dick and choke him with it."

Rachel smiles back. "I won't be long."

Then she turns to the prisoners cowering in the corner of the cell. Rachel knows that Addy won't be safe in this cell if she leaves these creatures alive. They are doomed to become the first victims of Rachel's wrath.

The girl in the sailor bikini beats them all to death with the anchor. As they wail and beg for mercy, she bashes their skulls into the ground one at a time, covering herself in their blood.

She slams her anchor down into their malnourished bodies until they are just a lump of meat on the floor. They still quiver and moan, wiggling their fingers and toes, even with their faces bashed in. Not quite able to die, but no longer able to see or hear or think or get off the ground ever again.

⚓

Blaise boards *The Pacific Princess*. After his daughter was captured and dragged onto the ship, he knew he couldn't leave her to such a horrific fate. A part of him wanted to go. A part of him wanted to leave her and save himself. He could have gotten away. The catapults were out of his reach. The cruise ship was moving in a direction that he could have avoided. They never would have found him. He could've gone back to safety, found help, and lived the rest of his life trying to forget the horrifying events that took place at sea.

But that's not the kind of person Blaise wants to be. He wants to be Daddy Cool. He thinks to himself, "What would Daddy Cool do?" And there's only one solution that echoes through his mind. If he truly was Daddy Cool he would get back on that ship, rescue his daughter and beat the shit out of all of those freaks who kidnapped her.

With only one spear left in his speargun, Blaise sneaks up the gangway onto the main deck of the ship. He's terrified. He doesn't know how to actually be a badass even though he likes to think of himself as one. If he's being honest with himself, he's just a sniveling wimp. He's always been a sniveling wimp. He was bullied by everyone when he was young. He's never had confidence in himself or any kind of strength to his character. Blaise just knows how to be Blaise. He hopes that will be enough.

He gets one look at Captain Stubing, standing on deck with his muscled chest and jagged meat cleaver, and decides maybe he made a terrible mistake. Maybe he really should have just rowed himself to safety and left his daughter to her fate. He doesn't even know if he's gotten on board fast enough. She could already be dead. And he thinks maybe he would have been better off not knowing what happened to her than witnessing for himself just what the mutants had in store for the young girl.

No matter how frightened he is, Blaise won't let himself give in to that fear. He won't run away. He didn't run away from being a father when Lily was born and he's not running away now. He keeps calling himself Daddy Cool in his brain and that's enough to keep him going.

"You're Daddy Cool," he says under his breath. "You've *got* this."

Daddy Cool wouldn't be afraid. Daddy Cool's afraid of NOTHING.

Blaise grips his speargun tightly, trying not to accidentally pull the trigger. His hands are shaking so much that he can't keep it steady. He takes a deep breath and then moves on.

Nothing is going to get in the way of Blaise saving his daughter. Not even himself.

⚓

Lily is surrounded by piles of rotten meat. Human limbs and torsos and random chunks of flesh lie like a pile of laundry at her feet. All of it is quivering and pulsing around her. She's never seen anything like it. She feels like she's hit some kind of jackpot.

When the mutants took her aboard, they were ready to gut her. The one in the Gopher mask wanted to slit her belly open and suck on her intestines. The doctor wanted to gouge her eyes out and fuck the sockets. But Lily was saved by the bartender, Isaac Washington. He stepped between them, ready to fight in order to save her from their depraved desires. The bartender explained in a series of grunts and squeals that she was not their prey. He told them that she was one of them.

The other mutants seemed skeptical. They couldn't imagine this frightened, whimpering girl could possibly find pleasure in the same sadistic acts as the rest of them. So they set up a test for her. They put her in a private cabin and filled it with flesh and body parts taken from their passengers.

The mutants stand in front of Lily, waiting to see how she reacts. Gopher, Isaac and Doc just watch her with their emotionless *Love Boat* faces. But Lily quickly proves the bartender right. She does not respond with disgust at the mountain of human flesh at all. Instead, she seems overjoyed. She's never received a gift so magnificent. She can't believe she'll be able to play with this meat to her heart's content.

"It's so beautiful!" Lily cries.

She can't believe the flesh is still moving. It's still alive and breathing with life. It is unlike any meat she's ever played with before.

Lily digs her hands into the pile of flesh and squeezes it. She falls into it and hugs it to her chest like a massive teddy bear. Then she proceeds to sculpt it into a castle. When she was young, she was very fond of building sand castles. She never thought she'd ever be able to build a sand castle out of living meat.

"It feels so good!" she yells, a giant smile on her face. "I can't believe there's so much meat!" She looks up at Isaac. "Is this mine? Can I keep it all?"

Isaac nods his head.

Lily giggles in excitement and continues to build her sand castle. She uses severed feet for the tops of towers and torsos as the base. Then she pulls all of the intestines out and molds them into a moat.

"This is so cool!" Lily says. "My mom and dad would never let me do this at home."

As she plays with the meat castle, Captain Stubing enters the room to find out what his crew is up to in here. They grunt and wheeze at him, explaining the situation. Despite his face hidden behind a metal plate, the captain is clearly moved by the little girl's passion. He can't help but fall in love with her. He kneels down and tries to help her build her sand castle, but Lily smacks his hand away.

She glares up at him in anger. "No! This is my meat!"

He just laughs and backs away, allowing her to have her fun.

The crew of *The Pacific Princess* has never seen such a wonderful girl. They've been looking for a child like her for a very long time, but have never been able to find one. The child passengers were always so frightened and disgusted by them. They gave them each a chance to prove themselves, but all of them ended up the same as the adult passengers. They all became their victims.

But Lily is different. She's special. They all know that she's a perfect match for them. They must have her join the crew. They must make her one of them.

⚓

When Lily is done with her meat castle, she leans back with a big smile on her face. The four mutants clap for her, giving her a round of applause. Lily has never seen anyone congratulate her on one of her works of art so much. She's never been more happy and proud.

"Isn't it great?" Lily asks. "I think it's my best meat work ever."

The mutants continue to clap. Lily stands up and bows. But they don't stop clapping. Their hands smack together loud and furiously, until blood appears in their hands.

The smile falls from Lily's face.

"What's wrong?" she asks them. "You really like it, don't you?"

Their claps are frightening the girl. It's like they are mocking her, as though they never liked the sculpture at all and were just laughing at her the whole time. She doesn't care how gruesome and terrifying the mutants are. She's more upset by the idea that they only pretended to like her artwork as a joke.

But when they finish clapping, they don't laugh. They don't ridicule her. Captain Stubing tears off a piece of his uniform and wraps it around a finger bone. Then he props it up on the top of Lily's castle, creating a little flag.

When Lily sees this, the smile returns to her face. "Oh yeah! That makes it even better!"

And then the captain goes to Lily and hugs her, pressing her tight to his chest. Even though he smells like rot, the little girl doesn't resist his embrace. She hugs him back, holding him tightly. She's never received such a loving embrace from anyone in her life. Not her mother or father. Not anyone. Lily has never known such comfort.

As tears roll down her cheek, Lily finds herself saying, "I love you, Captain Stubing!"

And the captain grunts at her in response, squeezing her tighter. Then he lifts her up off the ground and cradles her in his arms.

"Where are we going?" Lily asks, as the captain takes her out of the room.

Lily has no idea what they are doing as they take her to a dark room in the lower decks. It's the doctor's room. A place of torture and surgery, covered in blood and flesh. The captain places Lily on a table in the center of the room. She has no idea what's going on. A look of panic fills her eyes as they strap her down.

"What are you doing?" she cries.

But the mutants only wheeze at her. The doctor removes crude surgical tools from an old leather bag. When Lily sees him come at her with a rusty scalpel, she panics.

Captain Stubing hugs the girl, explaining to her with his love that everything is going to be alright. She doesn't have to be afraid. They just want to turn her into one of them.

But Lily is not comforted one bit. She resists the straps holding her down, pushing the captain away with her chest. Then she screams at the top of her lungs as the doctor pierces his scalpel into her cheek and cuts her open. He peels off her face like a band-aid and tosses it aside.

As Lily screams and begs for mercy, they show the girl her new face just before they put it on. It's a metal plate just small enough to fit on Lily's head. Glued to the front of the plate is a picture of an eleven-year-old girl from the 1970s. It is a picture of Vicki Stubing, the captain's daughter on *The Love Boat*, the character that the mutants expect her to become.

Lily can't do anything to stop them from transforming her. She wiggles and thrashes against her bonds as they put the plate to her face and drill holes into her skull, screwing the piece of metal into the bones of her face so that it will never be able to be removed ever again.

⚓
*

Rachel goes to the engine room and smashes all of the equipment with her thirty-pound anchor. She has no intention of allowing this vessel to move freely on the open seas ever again. These mutants need to be stopped. She will not permit them to continue their massacre across the ocean. Her first move is to ruin the ship. Then she plans to go after the crew.

The engines are left in steaming pieces by the time she's done with them, leaving the ship adrift. Then she waits for the mutants to come for her. She hides behind a wall of sound. The machines are squealing, hissing with steam. When the mutants come, they won't be able to hear her. Because they are unable to see, Rachel will be practically invisible to them.

Only one of the ship's crew goes downstairs to the engine room. It is Julie, the cruise director. She creeps into the room, grunting and rasping behind her metal mask. Her breasts cut open and splayed open like flowers. Her hook hand cutting into the side of her thigh in frustration. The mutant goes to the machinery, trying to figure out what is wrong. But it is too damaged for her to understand.

Rachel steps out from her wall of sound and lowers the anchor into the back of the mutant woman's neck, piercing through her spine. Julie falls to the ground and spins around. Then she swings her hook hand at Rachel. But the girl in the sailor bikini doesn't flinch. She lets the hook dig into her upper arm and then pulls on her anchor, throwing the cruise director over the back of her head.

The Julie mutant slams into a broken engine. Then Rachel swings her anchor again. She lowers it down into her forehead, hooking it beneath the metal face plate. Before the mutant can stop her, Rachel tears the mask off her face. The nails rip open her cheeks and bones, taking large chunks of meat with it. Blood gushes down the mutant's open breasts.

When Rachel gets a good look at the mutant woman without her mask, she sees exactly what the creatures are beneath the metal. Her face is without skin, without eyelids or lips or a nose. There are white orbs in the sockets where her eyes used to be, as though the irises melted away a long time ago.

The mutant screams and clutches at her face, feeling naked and exposed. She touches around the floor, searching for the mask. She's desperate to return it to her face, as though she is nothing without it. But without a care for her own wellbeing, she leaves herself wide open to another attack. Rachel stands over her and lifts the anchor as high as she can, then she bashes the mutant's skull open until its brains are scattered across the engine room floor.

Blaise saw Captain Stubing carrying his daughter away. Because he was with three other mutants, Blaise wasn't able to make his move. He just followed them below deck and waited outside the door. When he heard his daughter's screams, he just stood there, unable to do anything.

He knows something horrible is happening to her, but he can't get himself to take action. There's four of them and only one of him. He only has one spear for his speargun. He can't fight them unless it's one-on-one, and even then he doesn't know if he'd stand a chance. But his daughter is being hurt, maybe even tortured to death. He knows he can't just wait for the right moment to attack. It's either now or never.

As the sound of drilling continues, Blaise gets up the strength and courage to make his move. He peeks into the room and witnesses the mutants drilling a Vicki Stubing mask into his daughter's head. It fills him with disgust and anger. Not just because his daughter is being hurt, but because he always hated the character of Vicki Stubing. She ruined *The Love Boat* and was by far the worst character on the show. The idea that the mutants were turning his daughter into Vicki Stubing filled him with absolute rage. They've crossed a line and he won't let them get away with it.

Blaise bursts into the room and fires his spear into the back of the doctor's head. Then he runs at Captain Stubing and breaks his speargun against the side of the large mutant's neck.

"Daddy Cool in the house!" Blaise yells.

He feels like a badass for about a third of a minute. But then the mutants turn to him, not a single one of them fazed by his attack. He hears his daughter's muffled screams behind her metal mask, crying for help. And he's never felt more helpless in his life.

Completely unarmed and unable to protect himself, Blaise holds up his hands, trying to explain himself, as though it was all some kind of misunderstanding.

"Look, I didn't mean it, alright?" Blaise says, backing away. "Daddy Cool can admit when he's overstepped."

Then he turns and runs. There's no way he can save Lily at that moment. His only choice is to retreat.

The woman in the Gopher mask goes after him. She chases him down the hallway and jumps on him, pinning him to the ground. The other mutants just watch from the doorway of the surgery room.

Gopher glares down at him with her handsome man smile, holding Blaise's arms out and straddling him with her thighs. The smell of rancid fishy body odor fills Blaise's nostrils, as though she hasn't bathed in decades. Her greasy elongated breasts ooze over his throat and chest. She just stares at him, as though she can see him through her mask. Then she unzips his fly and grabs his dick.

Blaise has no idea what's going on. At first he thought she was going to kill him, but now he thinks she wants to fuck him. She pulls out his throbbing penis and strokes it, trying to get it hard. Blaise becomes awkward. He can't believe the mutant woman is trying to pleasure him like this, gurgling and moaning at him with excitement.

But instead of fucking him, the woman brings her knife toward his member and rubs the blade up his shaft. Blaise cries out, terrified of what she has planned. He struggles against her grip, using all of his strength to break free. But she's too strong. She holds both of his arms down with a single hand and Blaise is helpless.

Gopher smiles at Blaise with her friendly 1970s man smile as she toys with him, delicately scratching his penis against the tip of the knife.

"You fucking bitch," Blaise tells her. "Who do you think you're fucking with?"

His words excite the mutant even more. She cuts open his shirt and drops her knife on his belly so that she can touch him with her hand, digging into his flesh with her long dirt-caked fingernails, tearing thin cuts from his groin to his belly button.

"You're fucking with Daddy Cool, that's who," Blaise tells her.

Then his penis curls around the handle of the knife and stabs Gopher in the stomach.

⚓
*

Blaise has a very strange penis.

For most of his life, his penis was pathetic. It was very small and unremarkable. The kind of penis that gets lost in his bushy pubic hair. The kind of penis that made women break out in laughter whenever they saw it.

Blaise hated the fact that his penis was so small. It was the thing he hated most about himself. He would trade both of his legs and one arm for a large penis. He would rather die at forty if it meant having a decent-sized penis during his youth. It was his lifelong mission to try to correct this birth defect. When he made his fortune, he spent all the money he could on penis enlargement pills but nothing worked. Not until he heard about a new experimental surgery that was being explored in the Bangkok underground. He had a friend he sometimes did business with who admitted to having undergone such a surgery. He claimed that the doctors added eight inches to his penis, and it was the best decision he ever made in his life. Blaise had to know more. He had to correct the bane of his existence. So he cashed out his stocks and gathered up all of his money, then he flew across the world to get his penis fixed.

But when he met with the surgeons, he realized they were capable of doing so much more than extending the length of his member. They had the means to transplant muscle onto his dick, transforming it into much more than just a sex organ. After the surgery, Blaise's penis became like another arm. He was able to use it to hold glasses and lift up forks and spoons. It became like a baby elephant's trunk. He could move it freely, curling it around his girlfriend's wrist and pulling her into bed with him.

He was so fascinated by his new penis that he wanted to do more with it. He exercised it every day, pumping little weights to make his penis big and strong. Within two years, his dick had become a monster of bulbous muscle, stronger than even his own arms. He felt like a superhero. He felt like the manliest person on the face of the Earth. His penis was far superior to any other penis and it did more for his confidence than anything else ever could.

So when the mutant pinned Blaise to the ground and freed his penis from his pants, she had no idea what she was unleashing. Blaise's dick grabbed hold of her knife and cut her belly open.

The mutant is in shock as she sees the blade of her knife stuck inside of her. She has no idea how it even got there until Blaise's penis pulls the knife out, spins the blade around, and then stabs her again.

"You've just been Daddy Cooled!" Blaise yells at her.

She loosens her grip on his arms and Blaise breaks free. He gets to his feet and lunges his crotch at her face. His penis drives the knife into her throat and cuts through her esophagus. Then he slaps his penis back and forth across her face, scraping the blade of the knife against her metal mask. She reaches up, trying to grab his dick, but Blaise cuts up her fingers and then stabs the knife into the side of her temple.

The Love Boat picture of Gopher smiles up at Blaise as the mutant woman goes limp. She falls to the floor, splashing into a puddle of blood.

Then Blaise looks up at the other mutants, waving his penis

knife in their direction.

"Who's next?" Blaise yells. "Who wants to tangle with Daddy Cool?"

But the male mutants don't move. They decide it would be best not to tangle with Daddy Cool.

Before the mutants know how to react, Rachel comes up behind them and lowers her anchor into the doctor's back. One of the prongs breaks through his ribcage and exits out the front of his chest. Rachel doesn't care about the others. It's the doctor she wants. She pushes him to the ground and tears the anchor out of him, breaking open his chest and ripping out a lung. The doctor wheezes in pain, clutching the lung hanging out of his back. Rachel swings again, aiming for his leg. She smashes open his knee, popping the kneecap out of the joint, maiming him.

The bartender turns to her and grabs her with his muscular arms. He groans and yells, trying to crush her with his enormous strength. Rachel lets go of the anchor and grabs the large mutant by his wrists. Then she snaps them both like twigs. The bartender lets her go, his hands dangling limp. He has no idea how he'll be able to pour drinks now that his hands are useless noodles. But the thought doesn't last long. Rachel grabs the back of his head and pushes him to his knees. The parasites in her body squirm at full fury, pumping up the muscles in her arms to three times their size. Then she crushes his skull in her hand, popping it like a cantaloupe. His body drops to the ground. Then she looks over at Blaise.

Blaise gives her a thumbs up and says, "Good job, babe!"

Rachel sneers at him. "Fuck off, douchebag."

The last mutant standing doesn't know what to do. The great Captain Stubing has never been in such a position before.

On one side of him stands the grotesquely strong woman in a sailor bikini. On the other is the man waving a knife around with his weird penis. He has no other option. He decides to make a break for it.

Captain Stubing runs away. With the rest of his crew either dead or incapacitated, he has no choice but to try to save himself. He runs past Blaise and heads toward the front of the ship.

"Get him!" Rachel yells.

She charges after the captain. Blaise just lowers his penis knife and lets the Captain go past.

"Kill that son of a bitch!" Rachel says, running past Blaise.

But Blaise has no desire to go after the man. He takes the knife from his penis and returns his member to his pants. He zips himself up as he watches his ex-girlfriend chasing down the mutant with the anchor over her head.

Blaise goes back to the operating room to get his daughter. Lily is still strapped to the table, the picture of Vicki Stubing still drilled into her skull. Blaise can't stand to see his daughter in such a state. She's having difficulty breathing through the mask, moaning and whimpering at the pain.

"Daddy Cool's here, baby girl," he tells her, rushing to her side. "We took care of those mean people for you."

Lily whimpers and struggles against her bonds, almost more upset to be at the mercy of her douchebag father than the insane freaks. Blaise releases her from the straps and Lily sits up, grasping at the plate secured to her face.

"Let me help you with that," her father says.

He tries to pull the mask from her, but it's firmly attached. The screws go right into the bone.

"Shit…" Blaise says. "It's really stuck on there, isn't it?"

Lily tries to whine and complain through the mask, but her

words are too muffled for Blaise to understand.

"Let me get a screwdriver…" Blaise says.

He searches through the blood-caked tools on the ground until he finds a screwdriver. Then he goes back to his daughter.

"Okay, hold still," he tells her. "This might hurt a bit."

When Blaise attempts to unscrew one of the fasteners, Lily screams out in pain. She can feel the screw turning inside of her skull, scraping against the bone. She pushes her father back.

Blaise gets annoyed. "What do you expect me to do? I have to take it off even if it hurts. You don't want to be that annoying Vicki Stubing for the rest of your life, do you?"

He tries again but it only causes her more pain. She pushes him back, shaking her head.

"Do you want me to take it off or not?" Blaise says.

It's clear she would rather keep it on for now.

"Well, maybe we'll find some anesthetic around here somewhere…" Blaise says.

He looks around but there's nothing he can find that will help. He can't even give her pain pills with her mouth covered.

As Blaise scans the room for something to help his daughter, the doctor crawls into the room, whimpering and wheezing.

Blaise looks at the wounded mutant and says, "Hey, we're busy in here."

Then the mutant backs out of the room and crawls away.

⚓

Rachel chases Captain Stubing across the ship, but the mutant has nowhere to go. There's nowhere he can escape, even on such a large boat. The captain climbs down the gangway and finds Blaise's dinghy tied to the steps. He unravels the rope and hops down into the small vessel. Then he paddles himself away from *The Pacific Princess*.

"Where the fuck do you think you're going?" Rachel yells

down at him.

But the mutant keeps paddling, trying to get away from the terrifying woman.

"I'm not done with you yet," Rachel says. "I'm going to fuck you up when I get my hands on you."

The captain doesn't stop fleeing. He uses all of his strength to row himself far away from the cruise ship. Once he's out of range of the boat, he begins to spasm. His body thrashes in pain and then goes limp.

Rachel stares across the water at him, wondering what happened. The man just died out of nowhere. He floats away, toward the horizon. His body no longer moving.

"What the fuck was that?" Rachel asks, but the mutant is too far away to hear her.

The rowboat drifts off into the distance and disappears over the horizon. She isn't sure what happened, but it seems like the mutant has died. It's like he has been dead for a very long time and it was the ship itself that was keeping him alive.

Rachel goes down to the lowest deck of the ship and sees the crate filled with glowing crystals. She doesn't understand what they are, but she is sure they are the reason that she's still alive. For some reason, this strange mineral has the power to prolong life, no matter how damaged a person's body might become. It essentially has made them immortal for as long as they are within its proximity.

When she returns to Addy in her cell, Rachel discovers that her girlfriend is still wide awake and breathing. She almost looks like she's doing better than she was before. The strange glowing mineral has kept her going.

The two women embrace each other and Rachel explains that they're safe now. Then she stuffs Addy's intestines back into her body and helps her to her feet. She doesn't care how absurd the idea is that they can no longer die. As long as they're together, that's all that matters.

Rachel presses Addy's intestines tightly into her abdomen

and then hugs her, kissing her deeply.

When their lips part, Rachel tells her, "I'll love you forever."

Addy smiles at the woman of her dreams.

"We'll never, ever be apart."

And then they go upstairs, searching for a way to sew up Addy's stomach. Then they will wash themselves off, find a bed and make passionate love like no one ever has before. They nearly lost each other. Every second from here on out is a blessing. Nothing will ever keep them apart ever again.

EPILOGUE
DEREK

⚓

Derek wakes up at the bottom of the ocean. He has no idea why he is lying on the ocean floor or why his body has practically been cut in half. Why he's alive at all is an even bigger mystery. He's sure that one of the Conners had something to do with it. All of his other personalities are such morons. He hates every one of them. They could all die for all he cares, even though their death would mean his own.

Derek is not like the other personalities in Conner's body. He's the personality that rarely interacts with other people. He's the one who does most of Conner's homework. He's the only one who cleans their dorm room and plans for their future. He's the only responsible personality among them. This is why he calls himself Derek instead of Conner. The last thing he would want is to be compared to a Conner. They are all complete douchebags.

In his pocket, he finds a glowing orange crystal. Although he has no idea what it is, he can tell that it has something to do with why he is still alive. He puts it back into his pocket and then swims up to the surface.

Looking around, he sees nothing in sight. The ocean stretches for an eternity, but there are no boats or land for miles. He's not sure what to do. Just floating on the surface, treading water, he wonders if he shouldn't just let the crystal go and end it all. He has no problem letting the other Conners die. But he doesn't want to give up just yet. He knows that he was going on a sailing trip with his sister and her best friend and shithead sugar daddy. Although he hasn't spent much time directly with his sister, he does care for Rachel. He worries that she might be in trouble. He decides to keep himself alive for a little while longer. He would like to find her and make sure she's okay.

Not sure what else to do, Derek swims off, heading toward the horizon, hoping that he'll be able to be reunited with his sister once again.

⚓

It takes weeks before Derek finally finds *The Pacific Princess*. He comes across the derelict cruise ship as it floats adrift through the ocean waves. He knows that Conner boarded this ship, but isn't sure what happened there. Because none of the Conners have the strength to take over the body, Derek decides to climb aboard himself.

He's not sure what happened here, but the place is a mess. The deck is coated in blood. Body parts are spread out like loose laundry.

"Hello?" Derek calls out.

But there's nobody there. He's not sure how dangerous the place is. It seems like the kind of place that a maniac killer would call home.

He finds a young girl on the deck by the pool, sitting in front of a pile of human flesh. She is shredding the flesh in a small meat grinder, turning it into hamburger and using it like clay, combining it into a large sculpture. When Derek goes to the front of the child, he sees a metal plate attached to her face with the picture of *Love Boat* character Vicki Stubing attached to it. He can tell the girl is his sister's boyfriend's daughter, Lily.

But he has no idea what happened to her. Even though she can't see, she seems to have no problem sculpting and grinding her meat.

"Hey Lily, have you seen my sister?" Derek asks her.

The little girl just gurgles at him and continues her sculpture. He decides she won't be of any use to him so he moves on.

⚓

On the other side of the pool, Derek finds two people tied up on crucifixes. A man in a doctor's uniform and a shirtless woman with long dangling breasts. The two of them have been tortured well beyond death. They have no faces, as though their flesh has been removed with a shovel. They have been gutted and stabbed and cut apart. When Derek gets a closer look, he sees that they are still breathing. They are still alive. Somebody has been torturing them on what appears to be a daily basis. Their bodies are splayed open. Their guts on the ground below them. Their genitals have been mutilated. They are the most pitiful beings Derek has ever seen.

He moves on toward the front of the ship and sees a big sign that reads: DADDY COOL ZONE.

As Derek passes the sign, a man comes out from a corner, pointing a speargun at him.

"Did you read the sign?" the man asks. "This is Daddy Cool's zone. No one else allowed."

When Derek sees the man, he can't believe his eyes. Blaise has a full beard and long hair. He's shirtless with a horrible sunburn. His skin is pealing on his arms and chest. He seems like he's gone crazy. He's lost a lot of weight. He doesn't look anything like the man that was dating Derek's sister.

"Blaise?" Derek asks.

Blaise lifts his Daddy Cool sunglasses and is shocked to see him. "Conner? What the hell are you doing here?"

Even though Derek is not Conner, he doesn't correct the crazed man. He says, "I've been swimming for weeks. I finally found you."

"I thought you were dead," Blaise says, still aiming the speargun at him.

Derek nods. "I should be. What the hell happened here?"

Blaise looks him up and down. He doesn't like the sight of the college boy. He's been cut down the middle and half his body is hanging to the side. The sight of him frightens Daddy Cool. Blaise doesn't want to have anything to do with him.

"Just get the fuck back," Blaise tells him. "Go to the other side of the ship with all the other dead people."

"Is Rachel okay?" Derek asks.

Blaise shrugs. "She's one of them now. I'd stay the fuck away from that crazy bitch if I were you."

"She's my sister," Derek says.

"Not anymore," Blaise says.

Then the shirtless middle-aged man backs away, moving into the shadows to get out of the sun, still pointing his speargun at Derek with every step.

⚓

The ship is littered with skeletal zombie-like people. They were once the passengers on this cruise, but are now the walking dead. Somebody must have taken pity on them and let them free from their cages. Now they have the run of the ship. With their captors dead, they are no longer at their command. They are able to do as they please. Although most of them are lacking eyes and tongues, they still seem to be in good spirits despite their condition.

Derek looks behind him to see one of the zombie-like men wandering toward Blaise's area.

Blaise yells out, "Hey, this is Daddy Cool's area! Get out of here!"

Then the zombie wanders off in another direction.

⚓

Derek searches the ship top to bottom until he finally finds his sister in a master suite, curled up in bed next to her girlfriend, Addy. The two of them are practically melded together and appear to have not moved in days. Her body is boiling with movement, thousands of parasites crawling under her skin, eating her alive. Because the parasites are unable to die, they've been breeding inside of her at an alarming rate. She's no longer able to move, her muscles completely disintegrated. She's now more parasite than human on the inside. Her girlfriend isn't any better off than she is. The girl is barely conscious, holding Rachel close.

When his sister sees him, she can hardly believe her eyes. She doesn't have the strength to get up, but she smiles gently in his direction.

"Conner…" she says. "You came back."

Derek nods. "It took a long time to find you, but I finally made it."

He sits down on the bed next to her and puts his hand on her shoulder. He feels hundreds of fetus worms writhing under her skin.

"I'm glad you're okay," Rachel says.

Derek lifts his shoulder up, trying to put his torso back together. "I'm far from okay."

Rachel smiles. "Yeah. Neither are we."

"You look like you've been through hell," Derek says. "I'm sorry I wasn't here to help you. I'm a terrible brother."

Rachel shakes her head. "I'm your older sister. It's me that should have protected you."

Derek doesn't know what to say to her. As she tries to speak, a spool of fetus worms fills her mouth and causes her to gag. He can't believe the state she's in. She looks like she's in so much pain. She looks so miserable. He wishes he could help her.

"I love you, sis," he tells her, but she's unable to respond.

He leans in and hugs her. Then he stands up.

He says, "I'll fix this. I'll make everything better."

He looks down at her and sighs. Then he turns away.

"I'll let you rest in peace with your girlfriend, forever."

⚓

Derek goes to the dungeon of the ship and locates the crate filled with orange crystals. He wheels it up the stairs, lugging it to the top deck. It's the only thing he can think of to fix their situation. He has no desire to go on living and he hates the idea of his sister continuing in such a painful, miserable state. It's best to just end it all right now for all of them.

One at a time, he tosses the orange rocks overboard, starting with the one in his pocket. He has no idea where they came from or how they found their way aboard *The Pacific Princess*, but he knows they were not meant for human beings to find. He dumps all of the stones into the sea and watches them sink.

This will kill everyone on board. It will kill his sister and her girlfriend. It will kill all the zombie-like people and the mutants hanging on their crosses. It will kill the little girl. It will kill himself. Everyone on the ship except for Blaise will die. And he doesn't have a problem with that. They have all been killed already. It's time for them all to lie down and move on from this world.

Derek doesn't believe in Heaven, but he hopes he'll be able to see everyone again somewhere someday. He wonders if all of the Conners will be there, waiting for him on the other side. He wonders if his sister will forgive him for ending her life just because she appeared to be in so much pain. He wonders if he's a horrible person for letting the young girl die when she was having so much fun playing with her pile of meat. But as the stones sink to the bottom of the ocean, the life fades out of his eyes and he wonders no more.

⚓

When Blaise is finally rescued several months later, the Coast Guard finds him surrounded by dead bodies. He promises that he didn't kill any of them. He tells them that Daddy Cool would never do such a thing. But the state of everyone on board is so horrifying. They were all killed in such gruesome ways that the Coast Guard has a difficult time believing him, especially when so many of the bodies are filled with holes created from his speargun.

He tries to tell them about the mutants in *The Love Boat* masks. He tries to tell them about the glowing mineral that had kept them alive for decades. But even though they find it strange that the ship is the original *Pacific Princess* that was lost at sea in the early 1970s, they decide it would be best to arrest him and pin everything on the sole survivor.

"Daddy Cool's no killer!" Blaise cries as they take him away. "Daddy Cool's the man!"

But the Coast Guard is finished listening to him. They are too horrified by the scene on the cruise ship to take anything he says seriously. And every single one of them knows one thing for sure: Daddy Cool is going to be put behind bars for a very long time.

BONUS SECTION

This is the part of the book where we would have published an afterword by the author but he insisted on drawing a comic strip instead for reasons we don't quite understand.

"Thank you for reading my new book, *Apeship*. I hope you enjoyed it!"

It's me CM3!

"It's been a while since I've written a book in the world of Apeshit."

"The Apeshit series is always fun to write in and I always wanted to write an "Apeshit at sea" story, so that's why I wrote this book."

...

ape ship

What? Did you have a problem with it?
Yeah, I have a problem with the title.
ape ship
What the hell does Apeship even mean?
ape ship
It's a sequel to Apeshit and it takes place on a boat, so I called it Apeship.
Yeah, but Apeshit means something. It's slang for going violently crazy. It makes sense. Apeship does not.
ape ship

No, it makes sense. "Going ape" is also a thing, so if you "go ape" on a "ship" then the ship is an apeship.
But then it would be spelled two words: *Ape Ship*.
But your title is just one word.
ape ship
Well... What if it is like the word *friendship* or *followship*, but for people going ape together? An *Apeship*.
But you just said that it's called Apeship because it takes place on a boat...
ape ship
Then maybe it's a cool new slang term I invented.
When somebody goes apeshit while on a boat, they go apeship.
ape ship

The next book in the series is going to be called Spaceshit. And spaceshit is a term I made up for when somebody goes apeshit in space.
Then by that logic, the book should be called Boatshit. Not Apeship.
ape ship
Nah, that sounds too close to Boat Ship, which is the name of a book Vince Kramer came up with about a ship that is haunted by a ghost boat.
At least it would make sense. If I wrote a splatterpunk book set at sea, I'd call it Blood Ship or Splatter Ship or Death Sea or something like that.
ape ship
Splatter Ship?
Yeah, that's cool I guess....
ape ship

If you're a **NERD!!!**

I'll stick to Apeship, thank you very much!
APESHIP 4 LIFE
#1
Grandmaster of book titling
Best book title of the year award
Apeship tattoo
THE END

THE CM3 COLLECTOR'S LIBRARY

Signed limited edition hardcovers of your favorite books by Carlton Mellick III.

— SUBSCRIBE TODAY

www.carltonmellick.com/exclusive-hardcovers

ABOUT THE AUTHOR

Carlton Mellick III has made a living writing bizarro fiction novels to a cult audience for over twenty years. He was named one of the top forty genre fiction authors under the age of forty by The Guardian. His work has been translated into German, Spanish, Italian, Czech, Polish, Russian, Turkish, Persian, French and Japanese.

He lives on the Washington Coast with his wife, Rose, and his pet squirrel, Chuckles.

Visit him online at **www.carltonmellick.com**

ALSO FROM CARLTON MELLICK III AND
ERASERHEAD PRESS
www.eraserheadpress.com

QUICKSAND HOUSE

Tick and Polly have never met their parents before. They live in the same house with them, they dream about them every night, they share the same flesh and blood, yet for some reason their parents have never found the time to visit them even once since they were born. Living in a dark corner of their parents' vast crumbling mansion, the children long for the day when they will finally be held in their mother's loving arms for the first time... But that day seems to never come. They worry their parents have long since forgotten about them.

When the machines that provide them with food and water stop functioning, the children are forced to venture out of the nursery to find their parents on their own. But the rest of the house is much larger and stranger than they ever could have imagined. The maze-like hallways are dark and seem to go on forever, deranged creatures lurk in every shadow, and the bodies of long-dead children litter the abandoned storerooms. Every minute out of the nursery is a constant battle for survival. And the deeper into the house they go, the more they must unravel the mysteries surrounding their past and the world they've grown up in, if they ever hope to meet the parents they've always longed to see.

Like a survival horror rendition of *Flowers in the Attic*, Carlton Mellick III's *Quicksand House* is his most gripping and sincere work to date.

HUNGRY BUG

In a world where magic exists, spell-casting has become a serious addiction. It ruins lives, tears families apart, and eats away at the fabric of society. Those who cast too much are taken from our world, never to be heard from again. They are sent to a realm known as Hell's Bottom—a sorcerer ghetto where everyday life is a harsh struggle for survival. Porcelain dolls crawl through the alleys like rats, arcane scientists abduct people from the streets to use in their ungodly experiments, and everyone lives in fear of the aristocratic race of spider people who prey on citizens like vampires.

Told in a series of interconnected stories reminiscent of Frank Miller's *Sin City* and David Lapham's *Stray Bullets*, Carlton Mellick III's *Hungry Bug* is an urban fairy tale that focuses on the real life problems that arise within a fantastic world of magic.

STACKING DOLL

Benjamin never thought he'd ever fall in love with anyone, let alone a Matryoshkan, but from the moment he met Ynaria he knew she was the only one for him. Although relationships between humans and Matryoshkans are practically unheard of, the two are determined to get married despite objections from their friends and family. After meeting Ynaria's strict conservative parents, it becomes clear to Benjamin that the only way they will approve of their union is if they undergo The Trial—a matryoshkan wedding tradition where couples lock themselves in a house for several days in order to introduce each other to all of the people living inside of them.

SNUGGLE CLUB

After the death of his wife, Ray Parker decides to get involved with the local "cuddle party" community in order to once again feel the closeness of another human being. Although he's sure it will be a strange and awkward experience, he's determined to give anything a try if it will help him overcome his crippling loneliness. But he has no idea just how unsettling of an experience it will be until it's far too late to escape.

MOUSE TRAP

It's the last school trip young Emily will ever get to go on. Not because it's the end of the school year, but because the world is coming to an end. Teachers, parents, and other students have been slowly dying off over the past several months, killed in mysterious traps that have been appearing across the countryside. Nobody knows where the traps come from or who put them there, but they seem to be designed to exterminate the entirety of the human race.

Emily thought it was going to be an ordinary trip to the local amusement park, but what was supposed to be a normal afternoon of bumper cars and roller coasters has turned into a fight for survival after their teacher is horrifically killed in front of them, leaving the small children to fend for themselves in a life or death game of mouse and mouse trap.

NEVERDAY

Karl Lybeck has been repeating the same day over and over again, in a constant loop, for what feels like a thousand years. He thought he was the only person trapped in this eternal hell until he meets a young woman named January who is trapped in the same loop that Karl's been stuck within for so many centuries. But it turns out that Karl and January aren't alone. In fact, the majority of the population has been repeating the same day just as they have been. And society has mutated into something completely different from the world they once knew.

THE BOY WITH THE CHAINSAW HEART

Mark Knight awakens in the afterlife and discovers that he's been drafted into Hell's army, forced to fight against the hordes of murderous angels attacking from the North. He finds himself to be both the pilot and the fuel of a demonic war machine known as Lynx, a living demon woman with the ability to mutate into a weaponized battle suit that reflects the unique destructive force of a man's soul.

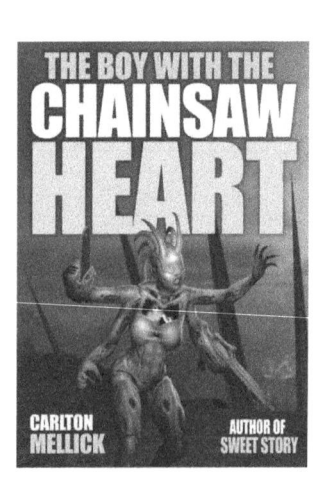

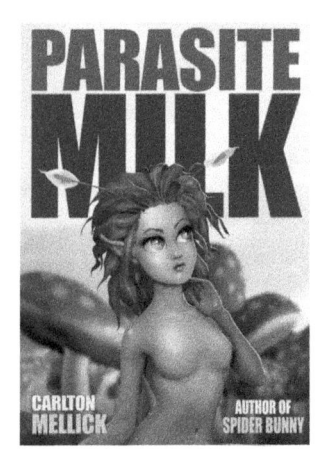

PARASITE MILK

Irving Rice has just arrived on the planet Kynaria to film an episode of the popular Travel Channel television series *Bizarre Foods with Andrew Zimmern: Intergalactic Edition*. Having never left his home state, let alone his home planet, Irving is hit with a severe case of culture shock. He's not prepared for Kynaria's mushroom cities, fungus-like citizens, or the giant insect wildlife. He's also not prepared for the consequences after he spends the night with a beautiful nymph-like alien woman who infects Irving with dangerous sexually-transmitted parasites that turn his otherworldly business trip into an agonizing fight for survival.

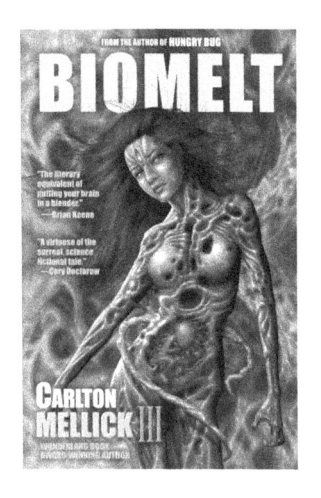

BIO MELT

Nobody goes into the Wire District anymore. The place is an industrial wasteland of poisonous gas clouds and lakes of toxic sludge. The machines are still running, the drone-operated factories are still spewing biochemical fumes over the city, but the place has lain abandoned for decades.

When the area becomes flooded by a mysterious black ooze, six strangers find themselves trapped in the Wire District with no chance of escape or rescue. Banding together, they must find a way through the sea of bio-waste before the deadly atmosphere wipes them out. But there are dark things growing within the toxic slime around them, grotesque mutant creatures that have long been forgotten by the rest of civilization. They are known only as clusters--colossal monstrosities made from the fused-together body parts of a thousand discarded clones. They are lost, frightened, and very, very hungry.

THE TERRIBLE THING THAT HAPPENS

There is a grocery store. The last grocery store in the world. It stands alone in the middle of a vast wasteland that was once our world. The open sign is still illuminated, brightening the black landscape. It can be seen from miles away, even through the poisonous red ash. Every night at the exact same time, the store comes alive. It becomes exactly as it was before the world ended. Its shelves are replenished with fresh food and water. Ghostly shoppers walk the aisles. The scent of freshly baked breads can be smelled from the rust-caked parking lot. For generations, a small community of survivors, hideously mutated from the toxic atmosphere, have survived by collecting goods from the store. But it is not an easy task. Decades ago, before the world was destroyed, there was a terrible thing that happened in this place. A group of armed men in brown paper masks descended on the shopping center, massacring everyone in sight. This horrible event reoccurs every night, in the exact same manner. And the only way the wastelanders can gather enough food for their survival is to traverse the killing spree, memorize the patterns, and pray they can escape the bloodbath in tact.

THE BIG MEAT

In the center of the city once known as Portland, Oregon, there lies a mountain of flesh. Hundreds of thousands of tons of rotting flesh. It has filled the city with disease and dead-lizard stench, contaminated the water supply with its greasy putrid fluids, clogged the air with toxic gasses so thick that you can't leave your house without the aid of a gas mask. And no one really knows quite what to do about it. A thousand-man demolition crew has been trying to clear it out one piece at a time, but after three months of work they've barely made a dent. And then there's the junkies who have started burrowing into the monster's guts, searching for a drug produced by its fire glands, setting back the excavation even longer.

It seems like the corpse will never go away. And with the quarantine still in place, we're not even allowed to leave. We're stuck in this disgusting rotten hell forever.

EVERY TIME WE MEET AT THE DAIRY QUEEN, YOUR WHOLE FUCKING FACE EXPLODES

Ethan is in love with the weird girl in school. The one with the twitchy eyes and spiders in her hair. The one who can't sit still for even a minute and speaks in an odd squeaky voice. The one they call Spiderweb.

Although she scares all the other kids in school, Ethan thinks Spiderweb is the cutest, sweetest, most perfect girl in the world. But there's a problem. Whenever they go on a date at the Dairy Queen, her whole fucking face explodes. He's not sure why it happens. She just gets so excited that pressure builds under her skin. Then her face bursts, spraying meat and gore across the room, her eyeballs and lips landing in his strawberry sundae.

At first, Ethan believes he can deal with his girlfriend's face-exploding condition. But the more he gets to know her, the weirder her condition turns out to be. And as their relationship gets serious, Ethan realizes that the only way to make it work is to become just as strange as she is.

EXERCISE BIKE

There is something wrong with Tori Manetti's new exercise bike. It is made from flesh and bone. It eats and breathes and poops. It was once a billionaire named Darren Oscarson who underwent years of cosmetic surgery to be transformed into a human exercise bike so that he could live out his deepest sexual fantasy. Now Tori is forced to ride him, use him as a normal piece of exercise equipment, no matter how grotesque his appearance.

SPIDER BUNNY

Only Petey remembers the Fruit Fun cereal commercials of the 1980s. He remembers how warped and disturbing they were. He remembers the lumpy-shaped cartoon children sitting around a breakfast table, eating puffy pink cereal brought to them by the distortedly animated mascot, Berry Bunny. The characters were creepier than the Sesame Street Humpty Dumpty, freakier than Mr. Noseybonk from the old BBC show Jigsaw. They used to give him nightmares as a child. Nightmares where Berry Bunny would reach out of the television and grab him, pulling him into her cereal bowl to be eaten by the demented cartoon children.

When Petey brings up Fruit Fun to his friends, none of them have any idea what he's talking about. They've never heard of the cereal or seen the commercials before. And they're not the only ones. Nobody has ever heard of it. There's not even any information about Fruit Fun on google or wikipedia. At first, Petey thinks he's going crazy. He wonders if all of those commercials were real or just false memories. But then he starts seeing them again. Berry Bunny appears on his television, promoting Fruit Fun cereal in her squeaky unsettling voice. And the next thing Petey knows, he and his friends are sucked into the cereal commercial and forced to survive in a surreal world populated by cartoon characters made flesh.

SWEET STORY

Sally is an odd little girl. It's not because she dresses as if she's from the Edwardian era or spends most of her time playing with creepy talking dolls. It's because she chases rainbows as if they were butterflies. She believes that if she finds the end of the rainbow then magical things will happen to her--leprechauns will shower her with gold and fairies will grant her every wish. But when she actually does find the end of a rainbow one day, and is given the opportunity to wish for whatever she wants, Sally asks for something that she believes will bring joy to children all over the world. She wishes that it would rain candy forever. She had no idea that her innocent wish would lead to the extinction of all life on earth.

Sweet Story is a children's book gone horribly wrong. What starts as a cute, charming tale of rainbows and wishes soon becomes a vicious, unrelenting tale of survival in an inhospitable world full of cannibals and rapists. The result is one of the darkest comedies you'll read all year, told with the wit and style you've come to expect from a Mellick novel.

AS SHE STABBED ME GENTLY IN THE FACE

Oksana Maslovskiy is an award-winning artist, an internationally adored fashion model, and one of the most infamous serial killers this country has ever known. She enjoys murdering pretty young men with a nine-inch blade, cutting them open and admiring their delicate insides. It's the only way she knows how to be intimate with another human being. But one day she meets a victim who cannot be killed. His name is Gabriel—a mysterious immortal being with a deep desire to save Oksana's soul. He makes her a deal: if she promises to never kill another person again, he'll become her eternal murder victim.

What at first seems like the perfect relationship for Oksana quickly devolves into a living nightmare when she discovers that Gabriel enjoys being killed by her just a little too much. He turns out to be obsessive, possessive, and paranoid that she might be murdering other men behind his back. And because he is unkillable, it's not going to be easy for Oksana to get rid of him.

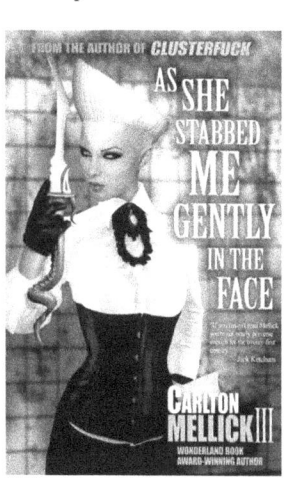

TUMOR FRUIT

Eight desperate castaways find themselves stranded on a mysterious deserted island. They are surrounded by poisonous blue plants and an ocean made of acid. Ravenous creatures lurk in the toxic jungle. The ghostly sound of crying babies can be heard on the wind.

Once they realize the rescue ships aren't coming, the eight castaways must band together in order to survive in this inhospitable environment. But survival might not be possible. The air they breathe is lethal, there is no shelter from the elements, and the only food they have to consume is the colorful squid-shaped tumors that grow from a mentally disturbed woman's body.

CUDDLY HOLOCAUST

Teddy bears, dollies, and little green soldiers—they've all had enough of you. They're sick of being treated like playthings for spoiled little brats. They have no rights, no property, no hope for a future of any kind. You've left them with no other option-in order to be free, they must exterminate the human race.

Julie is a human girl undergoing reconstructive surgery in order to become a stuffed animal. Her plan: to infiltrate enemy lines in order to save her family from the toy death camps. But when an army of plushy soldiers invade the underground bunker where she has taken refuge, Julie will be forced to move forward with her plan despite her transformation being not entirely complete.

ARMADILLO FISTS

A weird-as-hell gangster story set in a world where people drive giant mechanical dinosaurs instead of cars.

Her name is Psycho June Howard, aka Armadillo Fists, a woman who replaced both of her hands with living armadillos. She was once the most bloodthirsty fighter in the world of illegal underground boxing. But now she is on the run from a group of psychotic gangsters who believe she's responsible for the death of their boss. With the help of a stegosaurus driver named Mr. Fast Awesome—who thinks he is God's gift to women even though he doesn't have any arms or legs--June must do whatever it takes to escape her pursuers, even if she has to kill each and every one of them in the process.

VILLAGE OF THE MERMAIDS

Mermaids are protected by the government under the Endangered Species Act, which means you aren't able to kill them even in self-defense. This is especially problematic if you happen to live in the isolated fishing village of Siren Cove, where there exists a healthy population of mermaids in the surrounding waters that view you as the main source of protein in their diet.

The only thing keeping these ravenous sea women at bay is the equally-dangerous supply of human livestock known as Food People. Normally, these "feeder humans" are enough to keep the mermaid population happy and well-fed. But in Siren Cove, the mermaids are avoiding the human livestock and have returned to hunting the frightened local fishermen. It is up to Doctor Black, an eccentric representative of the Food People Corporation, to investigate the matter and hopefully find a way to correct the mermaids' new eating patterns before the remaining villagers end up as fish food. But the more he digs, the more he discovers there are far stranger and more dangerous things than mermaids hidden in this ancient village by the sea.

I KNOCKED UP SATAN'S DAUGHTER

Jonathan Vandervoo lives a carefree life in a house made of legos, spending his days building lego sculptures and his nights getting drunk with his only friend—an alcoholic sumo wrestler named Shoji. It's a pleasant life with no responsibility, until the day he meets Lici. She's a soul-sucking demon from hell with red skin, glowing eyes, a forked tongue, and pointy red devil horns... and she claims to be nine months pregnant with Jonathan's baby.

Now Jonathan must do the right thing and marry the succubus or else her demonic family is going to rip his heart out through his ribcage and force him to endure the worst torture hell has to offer for the rest of eternity. But can Jonathan really love a fire-breathing, frog-eating, cold-blooded demoness? Or would eternal damnation be preferable? Either way, the big day is approaching. And once Jonathan's conservative Christian family learns their son is about to marry a spawn of Satan, it's going to be all-out war between demons and humans, with Jonathan and his hell-born bride caught in the middle.

KILL BALL

In a city where everyone lives inside of plastic bubbles, there is no such thing as intimacy. A husband can no longer kiss his wife. A mother can no longer hug her children. To do this would mean instant death. Ever since the disease swept across the globe, we have become isolated within our own personal plastic prison cells, rolling aimlessly through rubber streets in what are essentially man-sized hamster balls.

Colin Hinchcliff longs for the touch of another human being. He can't handle the loneliness, the confinement, and he's horribly claustrophobic. The only thing keeping him going is his unrequited love for an exotic dancer named Siren, a woman who has never seen his face, doesn't even know his name. But when The Kill Ball, a serial slasher in a black leather sphere, begins targeting women at Siren's club, Colin decides he has to do whatever it takes in order to protect her... even if he has to break out of his bubble and risk everything to do it.

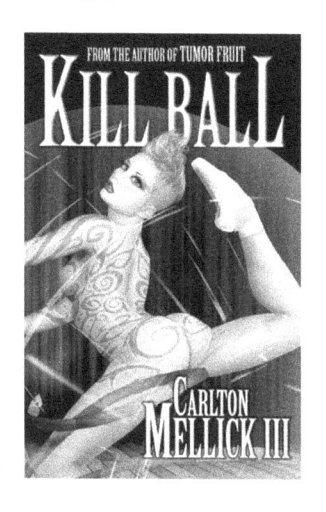

THE TICK PEOPLE

They call it Gloom Town, but that isn't its real name. It is a sad city, the saddest of cities, a place so utterly depressing that even their ales are brewed with the most sorrow-filled tears. They built it on the back of a colossal mountain-sized animal, where its woeful citizens live like human fleas within the hairy, pulsing landscape. And those tasked with keeping the city in a state of constant melancholy are the Stressmen- a team of professional sadness-makers who are perpetually striving to invent new ways of causing absolute misery.

But for the Stressman known as Fernando Mendez, creating grief hasn't been so easy as of late. His ideas aren't effective anymore. His treatments are more likely to induce happiness than sadness. And if he wants to get back in the game, he's going to have to relearn the true meaning of despair.

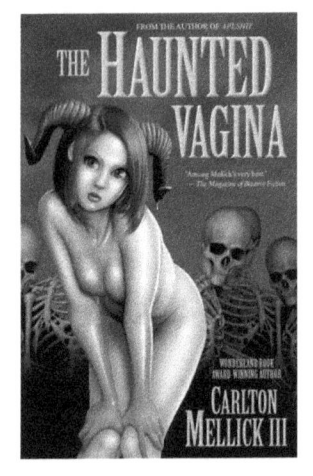

THE HAUNTED VAGINA

It's difficult to love a woman whose vagina is a gateway to the world of the dead...

Steve is madly in love with his eccentric girlfriend, Stacy. Unfortunately, their sex life has been suffering as of late, because Steve is worried about the odd noises that have been coming from Stacy's pubic region. She says that her vagina is haunted. She doesn't think it's that big of a deal. Steve, on the other hand, completely disagrees.

When a living corpse climbs out of her during an awkward night of sex, Stacy learns that her vagina is actually a doorway to another world. She persuades Steve to climb inside of her to explore this strange new place. But once inside, Steve finds it difficult to return... especially once he meets an oddly attractive woman named Fig, who lives within the lonely haunted world between Stacy's legs.

THE CANNIBALS OF CANDYLAND

There exists a race of cannibals who are made out of candy. They live in an underground world filled with lollipop forests and gumdrop goblins. During the day, while you are away at work, they come above ground and prowl our streets for food. Their prey: your children. They lure young boys and girls to them with their sweet scent and bright colorful candy coating, then rip them apart with razor sharp teeth and claws.

When he was a child, Franklin Pierce witnessed the death of his siblings at the hands of a candy woman with pink cotton candy hair. Since that day, the candy people have become his obsession. He has spent his entire life trying to prove that they exist. And after discovering the entrance to the underground world of the candy people, Franklin finds himself venturing into their sugary domain. His mission: capture one of them and bring it back, dead or alive.

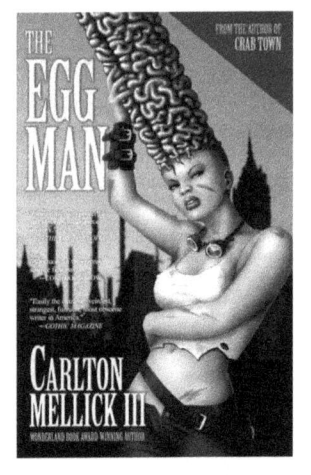

THE EGG MAN

It is a survival of the fittest world where humans reproduce like insects, children are the property of corporations, and having a ten-foot tall brain is a grotesque sexual fetish.

Lincoln has just been released into the world by the Georges Organization, a corporation that raises creative types. A Smell, he has little prospect of succeeding as a visual artist. But after he moves into the Henry Building, he meets Luci, the weird and grimy girl who lives across the hall. She is a Sight. She is also the most disgusting woman Lincoln has ever met. Little does he know, she will soon become his muse.

Now Luci's boyfriend is threatening to kill Lincoln, two rival corporations are preparing for war, and Luci is dragging him along to discover the truth about the mysterious egg man who lives next door. Only the strongest will survive in this tale of individuality, love, and mutilation.

APESHIT

Apeshit is Mellick's love letter to the great and terrible B-horror movie genre. Six trendy teenagers (three cheerleaders and three football players) go to an isolated cabin in the mountains for a weekend of drinking, partying, and crazy sex, only to find themselves in the middle of a life and death struggle against a horribly mutated psychotic freak that just won't stay dead. Mellick parodies this horror cliché and twists it into something deeper and stranger. It is the literary equivalent of a grindhouse film. It is a splatter punk's wet dream. It is perhaps one of the most fucked up books ever written.

If you are a fan of Takashi Miike, Evil Dead, early Peter Jackson, or Eurotrash horror, then you must read this book.

CLUSTERFUCK

A bunch of douchebag frat boys get trapped in a cave with subterranean cannibal mutants and try to survive not by using their wits but by following the bro code...

From master of bizarro fiction Carlton Mellick III, author of the international cult hits Satan Burger and Adolf in Wonderland, comes a violent and hilarious B movie in book form. Set in the same woods as Mellick's splatterpunk satire Apeshit, Clusterfuck follows Trent Chesterton, alpha bro, who has come up with what he thinks is a flawless plan to get laid. He invites three hot chicks and his three best bros on a weekend of extreme cave diving in a remote area known as Turtle Mountain, hoping to impress the ladies with his expert caving skills.

But things don't quite go as Trent planned. For starters, only one of the three chicks turns out to be remotely hot and she has no interest in him for some inexplicable reason. Then he ends up looking like a total dumbass when everyone learns he's never actually gone caving in his entire life. And to top it all off, he's the one to get blamed once they find themselves lost and trapped deep underground with no way to turn back and no possible chance of rescue. What's a bro to do? Sure he could win some points if he actually tried to save the ladies from the family of unkillable subterranean cannibal mutants hunting them for their flesh, but fuck that. No slam piece is worth that amount of effort. He'd much rather just use them as bait so that he can save himself.

THE BABY JESUS BUTT PLUG

Step into a dark and absurd world where human beings are slaves to corporations, people are photocopied instead of born, and the baby jesus is a very popular anal probe.

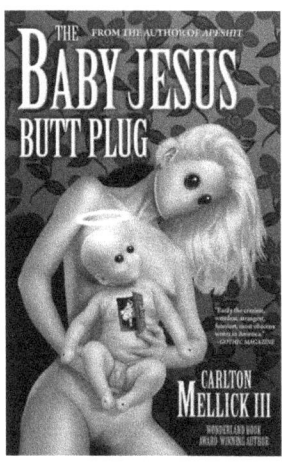

Milton Keynes UK
Ingram Content Group UK Ltd.
UKHW012321110424
440929UK00001B/45